YOU MUST BELIEVE ME!

Janet Kay Gallagher

Publishing Coordinator – Sharon Kizziah-Holmes

WINTER LAKE
PRESS

ISBN -13: 978-1-956806-15-1

DEDICATION

This book is dedicated to my brother Robert Stanton Whittaker McNabb. Bob was an avid reader and enjoyed Mystery, Suspense, Crime Drama, and True Crime.

ACKNOWLEDGMENTS

In 2009 I attended a writing group lead by Nicholas Inman. When he got a full-time job at the Marshfield Mail Newspaper, he asked me to take over the group and keep it going. I have been leading that group and in 2019 we our celebrated our 10-year Anniversary, our current name is THE QUILL AND INK WRITERS. Special thanks to currant members, Myrtle DeLaney, Mitch DeLaney, Ruby Joyce, Anita Keeling, Claudette Smith, Carolyn Moye, Betty Jo Cantrell, and Melissa Mall. I am thankful for all who have attended over the years and listened to my stories and gave feedback. Special Remembrance of Charles Christman, and Elsie Myers who were original member, who have passed.

I needed to learn about writing so I attended a Book Signing in Springfield, Missouri that was associated with the 2009 ORA WRITERS CONFERENCE. I met the authors who were speaking at the conference. And best yet I met members of the local writing groups, OZARKS ROMANCE AUTHORS, SLEUTH'S INK MYSTERY WRITERS, OZARKS WRITERS LEAGUE AND SPRINGFIELD WRITERS GUILD.

I was so impressed with the people I met that day, that I joined all the groups.

I met Cait London, one of my long-time favorite authors, who lived in Branson and belongs to the ORA group. Sharon Kizziah-Holmes who is my publisher/encourager. Shirley McCann smiles and brightens the world. She told me to, write, edit, submit and do it again. Barbara Bettis, Nancy Dailey, V.J. Schultz, Ruth Hunter, Rose Lombardo, Susan Keene and I know I have left out some. I want everyone in these groups to know I am glad to call you friend and that each of you has played a part in my writing success.

Special Thanks to Susan Keene and Tierney James who drove me to Springfield Writers meetings with them. You have shared friendship, knowledge and encouragement with me.

You will find wonderful hours of reading enjoyment by checking out the names listed on this page as they are authors to add to your: TO READ LIST.

CHAPTER 1

The hard wooden chair in the police station caused Jonathan Perkins to fidget, he couldn't sit still. His fragile bones ached. He'd told them his story over and over and they didn't believe him. He was frightened and being treated like an idiot. He told Detective Andrew Palmer, "I know you don't believe me because I drink, but you must believe I saw that child grabbed off the street and pulled into a van."

Andy in his years in law enforcement had seen his share of homeless drunks wanting to get off the street awhile. They'd come in and tell some wild story and get the officers to put them up in an alcohol unit for a few days. Their benefit is good food, a warm dry place, and better drugs than they got outside.

This old guy's story was a little wilder than most

they heard. Mr. Perkins told them he'd seen a parochial schoolgirl abducted and pulled into a van. The cop he flagged down, almost believed it.

Andy knew Jonathan Perkins would under-go tests and be treated and released. Andy hated the paperwork and the tedium of these nights. He would go make the arrangements.

"Bob, keep an eye on the old geezer while I make the arrangements for his stay at the patient facility. I'll be back in a minute," Palmer murmured to his partner.

He headed down the hall to the computer office where he knew they would have good fresh coffee made by someone who knew how to make real coffee. *Who is working tonight?* He hoped it was Jean. She had been a widow about three years. He'd planned to ask her out to dinner and a movie.

"Hi, Sheila I need coffee, it's been a long tiring shift," he greeted as he passed her desk and went to the coffee area. He poured coffee into the ceramic mug with his name on it. Then returned to her and asked, "Is Jean working tonight?"

"Hi, Andy." She shook her head and continued adding new data into the system.

Disappointed he had missed talking to dispatcher Jean Baughman, Andy took the big mug and started to his desk. He stopped in a small office, not being used at this hour, and made the necessary phone calls to get Jonathan Perkins put in the Alcohol Unit.

He arrived back in his work area and saw that Jonathan was telling everyone about the young girl he saw get snatched. The officers were all in agreement that he was a regular old drunk, telling his pink elephant stories.

Andy heard the old man repeat over and over, "Did you find out who those criminals were, the guys that took her? Are you out there looking for them? Will she be, ok? You must believe me! I saw two white men, maybe twenties, one with dark hair and the other with odd blue in his hair. They were in a gray or silver van, and they opened the sliding door and pulled her inside. She was screaming, scared, so little and needs protection. You gotta help her."

Andy backed out of the room. He had been hearing it for the last five or more hours. He entered the bathroom, and decided it was a good idea to stay away from the old man right now. *How long can I hide out in here before someone comes looking for me*? Almost an hour went by and Andy knew the attendants would be getting there to pick up the drunk. *Better get back.*

His shift was almost over. He had checked the updated missing list, to make sure, and saw that no schoolgirl was on it. When the white coats showed themselves, Jonathan was extremely agitated. It took a lot of effort for the attendants to move him along.

"You must believe me! I did see a little girl taken by force! You have to help her!" he shouted again as they led him down the long hallway and out of the building.

Bob, came over to Andy's desk and said, "What if the old drunk really saw a child abducted? Did you even run the partial license he gave you?

Maybe she just hasn't been reported missing yet?"

"Look, Bob, I know you mean well, but I have been doing my job very well for many years. I know what I'm doing. My judgment call is DRUNK TRYING TO GET ATTENTION. And now he is getting it." Andy put finger quotes as he said this.

He debated whether to tell Bob why he knew so well. He decided he should since Bob didn't seem convinced. He cleaned off his desk as he stated, "My dad was an alcoholic and I have seen it all. You can't trust any of them. Lie, cheat, steal, spend every dollar they get on booze, is their way of life. Waste and ruin left all around them. Our shift is over." He stood and waved as he headed out the door. "See ya. I'm off for three days and I'm going to enjoy them.""

CHAPTER 2

When Andy answered his phone, he heard a familiar voice.

"Hi Andy, this is Captain Johnson, I'm sorry to call you in on your last day off but I need you to meet me at the Morgue. A young girl has been brought in. She was found in a dumpster near Franklin Street Bridge. I'm on my way. Get there as soon as you can," he said gruffly.

"Okay, Captain." Andy answered quietly.

Why did the man say Captain Johnson, not Brad? This was bad. In all the years they had worked together, Bradley had never announced himself as Captain Johnson. Oh, no it couldn't be the girl that old man told him and the rest of the departmet about. Andy was so sure he didn't have any idea what he was jabbering about. It had to be someone else. He'd checked the latest missing list before coming back home.

Where are those socks? He had to hurry. They might fire him. If so, he would probably lose his pension. Andy had worked hard too many years for that to happen this late in his career.

He had a good, clean, even honored record. What would happen? He'd lose everything, house, car, insurance, and medical. What if he got sued?

What was wrong with him? Thinking about his problems when a little girl had lost her life at the hands of the worst kind of criminals. And then she had been thrown away like trash in a dumpster. How devastating that will be for her parents. Andy felt sick but he had to get to the morgue.

When he pulled into the parking lot he noted the grim look on Brad's face. The captain was waiting for him. Andy parked his car and got out. "Hi Brad," Andy said.

"Let's go. Keep your mouth shut. We'll talk when we come out. Is that clear?"

"Yes, sir."

Entering the Morgue was everyone's least favorite thing to do. It meant someone was dead and usually another person was responsible. In this case the detective didn't want to be in this spot.

As they walked the hallway in silence Andy thought about his life. He had been a highly respected cop, doing everything by the book, even when it hurt to do so for fourteen or fifteen years? These days it all ran together. If he let that child down, how could he live with the guilt and utter humiliation? His good judgment questioned at every turn by all who work with him, and especially his own ability to trust himself.

As soon as he saw the white blouse and navy tartan plaid jumper her catholic school uniform on the table beside the body being examined by the coroner, he knew the horrible truth. Andy wanted to cry but knew he had better keep it all together. He had allowed his personal feelings to get in the way of his job. If he had followed the leads given by that old drunk, this might not have been the outcome. They might have been able to save this child. If only he had acted fast enough. Put out the amber alert. And followed through on the partial license plate number.

How could he ever forgive himself for letting this child down. She had been beaten, raped, and left in a dumpster. He had noted the white bow still in her dark hair. How can her face be bruised and discolored and still look beautiful and angelic?

The coroner interrupted Andy's thoughts by saying, "Brad thanks for coming in this morning with Mrs. Morrow when she identified this child as her ten-year old daughter Dana Morrow. Watching parents identify their loved ones is the worst part of my job as coroner."

Brad said, "She really took it hard. I hope she can handle it. I put her in contact with some people who have been through this too and maybe that will help."

Finally, Brad thanked the coroner and started out the door. They walked that long hallway again, still in silence.

Andy practiced regulated breathing on the way out of there. It had been difficult to get enough air in the odiferous room the coroner was using today, and hard here too. When they got outside, they both took in big gulps of fresh air.

Brad spoke, "Mrs. Morrow came into the precinct the next morning after you spoke to Jonathan Perkins, to report her missing daughter, Dana Morrow. She worked the night shift at the Langston Building in the cleaning crew. When she got home about four-thirty A.M. she found out Dana was missing. She searched the neighbors, and the area around their apartment building. Then she came to us.

Andy, I put you on a thirty-day vacation. You had plenty of leave time you hadn't taken. You made a bad call. I made you look at her so you will never forget, the missing schoolgirl case you didn't follow-up. Bob will take the leads you had and work them as if they just came into us. We're hoping, he can still solve this murder. And pray that after the detox your drunk has forgotten what he told you. Bob is not happy with you right now, but he will help save your career. This decision is not mine alone. We didn't want to have to send this to Case Review and Internal Affairs. So, keep your mouth shut, take the time, and come back the cop you have always made me respect. Or turn in your badge."

"Ok, thanks for standing by me. I'm ashamed and deeply troubled that I didn't do all I could to find that girl. I was positive that old guy was so drunk he was seeing things and wanted to find a warm spot for the night."

Brad nodded, and continued, "You're scheduled

to see Doctor Allen Breen next Tuesday at 2 P.M. I'll send the address by e-mail. This is mandatory. Also, you will attend Al-Anon Meetings at Faith Church, Tuesday, and Thursday nights. These are not associated with the department, so these requirements won't be known by anyone else. Andy, use this time to get yourself back on track. God can help you with this if you let him." As he got into his car he added, "See you in church."

Stunned and ashamed, Andy sat in his car. He didn't feel like going anywhere. So, he sat there in his dazed condition, closed his eyes and sobbed leaning over the steering wheel. All he could think about was the face of little Dana, laying on the morgue table, how he had failed her by allowing his personal feelings to cloud his judgment and prevent him from helping her. Andy didn't know how long he had been in his car, it seemed like hours, but it could have been a few minutes. He vowed to do right by tiny Dana and put her killers away.

His friends were going to cover for him in this foul up, but they may never give him another important case. Looks like Bob, just got promoted to Andy's previous position in the department. He can do it, but that's where Andy should be and was until, he let his personal life intrude on his career. Strive to be the best policeman/detective had always been his goal. He was good at his job, and was careful, organized, persistent, brave, trustworthy...until this little girl Dana Morrow's death.

As he drove home he remembered he needed food in the house to eat. The fast-food drive-thru window would take away the hunger so he could go into the grocery store and not buy everything in sight. Late night TV shows gave this as advice on all weight loss programs. People who forget and go to the store on an empty stomach don't lose the weight and spend more money than they planned.

In the tortilla aisle an old friend, Barbara said, "Hi Andy, what have you been doing lately? It seems like forever since I have run into you. Jimmy is three now and it seems I left the picture book at home," she said, as she rummaged in her giant handbag. "He's home with Jack. When are you going to come over for cards again? That nice girl you brought last time, are you still seeing her?"

"No." he told the short woman in front of him. "It has been a long time. Maybe we can get together soon, ok?" he said.

"Should I call you or you call us?" she remarked.

"I'll call you, I have a lot going on right now. But, I'll look forward to seeing you and Jack again, and the baby." he started down the aisle before she could speak again.

The world is falling apart and yet, everyday stuff continues. He still needed to eat, shop for groceries, and talk to old friends like everything is ok. It's good that no one can look inside you. They don't need to see the jelly you have become thinking about today's events. The checkout girl smiles and expects you to smile back. If you don't, they think you're rude. Life goes on. Everyone says that and it's true. But it doesn't help the grief when you have a tender loss. These events dull with time, but never completely remove themselves from our hearts.

He came into his house and did the necessary chores. He put the food away, checked through the mail and took care of the messages left on his phone. Then he picked up and straightened the house.

This was unheard of for him to go to bed this early, but today, that was the only relief he could think about. Sleep would keep the pain away for a while. Andy knew it was a sign of depression to want to sleep to block out the world and what was happening in one's life. But for now, that was the plan. Tomorrow, he would have to find a new and better way to cope. For the next three days, he slept, ate, then turned on the television for noise, and slept with it on, not noticing one day from another. Time stretched out and he was oblivious.

CHAPTER 3

Brad called on Tuesday morning to remind him of his appointment this afternoon. He heard the message being recorded, but didn't pick up the line. He took his time stretching and getting out of bed. His numb phase was over. He would have to pull himself together and face the outside world again. Wallowing in self-pity was not his way, usually.

The person who looked at him in the mirror was a bum! How could a beard grow that fast and ugly? It was the nice brown color of his hair, but very scraggly. *Will the electric razor even cut it?* That sent him looking for the scissors. *Do people know how hard it is to be clean shaven? No wonder all the pictures of cowboys, western men, miners and such wore beards. Maybe, if they grow for a couple months, they can just be trimmed and look good.* He couldn't imagine it, not for him. He trimmed his hair, shaved, and took a shower. At last, he looked like himself, again. Some thought he was good looking. No one had ever used the term handsome. Andy dressed with care for his appointment. He glanced in the mirror again and thought he might look a little older today. Had this tragedy already affected him that much, or had it crept up without his notice?

He booted up the computer to check e-mail, so many! Andy had to go through them to find the one Brad sent with instructions. Printed both, the doctor appointment this afternoon and Al-Anon meeting time and location for tonight.

He'd have time to stop somewhere for lunch. Alexander's was always a good place for a hearty meal, and after the last few days, maybe that's what he needed. As soon as he was seated, Martin the owner came over to talk. "Ok if I set down with you?" he asked.

"Sure, as always. What is today's special?" Andy asked.

"Rib Eye with roasted potatoes, and green beans with garlic bread." he replied.

"Sold, I'm hungry and have a 2 P.M. appointment," Andy said.

Martin gave the chef the order and returned. He set down two cups of hot black Espresso Double Shots, then slid into the booth.

"How is it going with the little girl they found a few days ago? Wow, the news is sure all over it. With those kinds of happenings, I sometimes wonder how you guys get any work done with the press after you all the time?" he shook his head and sipped his coffee.

"I have some time off and Bob Simon is working that case. I think you know him," Andy said.

Martin nodded, affirmative. Then said, "I wondered why he was answering the tough questions instead of you. How is the vacation? Do you still see the cute redhead?"

"No, on the redhead, catching up on some sleep" Andy lied. Not really a lie, since he had slept a lot, but not like the restful vacation sleep either. It felt like a lie, however. He shrugged it off. No one can know the truth. They carried on a lively conversation until the food arrived.

Martin said, "I better get back to business." and went back to his office down the short hallway by the kitchen.

The food was delicious as always, but it was hard to eat, as he thought about the news coverage he had missed, since he kept the radio and television off the news channels. Movies and Sci-Fi gave lots of noise, but no news. The news teams with cameras, would have been to the crime scene dumpster. Had a shot outside the coroner's office, talking with the child's parents, relatives, and friends. They would stand outside the police station and ask what the police were doing to find the murderer. And put the pressure on, making up some fill questions that stirred up everyone and sometimes made it harder for the police to do their job. If the reporter was aggressive, they might find someone that hadn't been interviewed by the authorities yet. Then their story was set by the time the cop got to them and any helpful information might be gone.

The captain had been right. He would never forget the little child, Dana Morrow. With her beautiful face battered, and her lip bloody and swollen from a hit or two. The burgundy plaid uniform would always be there in his mind. Could he ever be an effective cop again or has he ruined his life, as well as, getting Dana killed? He'd better get to the appointment with Doctor Breen.

Andy paid for lunch, and then drove to the doctor's office. The traffic was lighter than usual. He arrived a few minutes early, which was good since there would be paperwork to fill out as a new patient.

"Hello, I have a two o'clock appointment with Doctor Allen Breen. My name is Andrew Palmer."

"Mr. Palmer, would you please fill out the papers on the clipboard and return it to me when you finish" she quietly requested.

Taking the papers to a nearby comfortable chair, he sat down. Lush surroundings, muted lavender walls with accents of the exactly right shade of blue green. A fashionable décor was displayed, throughout. It was all very soothing to the eyes and mind. The doctor must make a bundle of dough!

Andy returned the papers to the elegant older woman with the muted voice and silvery hair. She was perfectly suited to her surroundings.

"Please be seated and the doctor will be with you shortly. Would you like a cup of coffee while you wait?" she intoned.

"No thanks, I just came here from lunch," he said.

Forty-five minutes later he was still waiting, and he was tired of it.

"The doctor will see you now," she announced. "Go through that door and turn left." Dr. Allen Breen was short, a bit round. and wore horned rimmed glasses that hadn't been in style for years, and he looked so out of place, in the wonderfully decorated room.

They must have designed these offices for women, with pretty flowers, nice colors, and soft comfortable chairs with ottomans. Maybe this man is a leftover patient that hasn't left yet. *Did I open the wrong door? No, I went left.*

"Are you Dr. Breen?"

"Who else would I be? I'm sitting here waiting for Andrew Palmer."

"That's me; do you know why I'm here?" Andy asked.

"Young man, do you know, why you're here?

"I think the department sent me to see if I'm ok"

"What department? Do you think you're ok?" he asked.

They sent me to a crazy person! This is going to take a long time. He wanted out of here. Help! Is this how psychologists are supposed to act?

"I get paid by the hour so, if you don't want to talk that's ok by me young man."

"Okay, Doc what do we talk about? I'm new to this."

"Tell me anything about yourself that you want to."

"I'm a cop, detective now, and I want to continue doing my job. I'm good at it, and it's my career choice. I have done it very well for many years and been respected."

"Did something happen that you can't continue?"

"That's the million-dollar question! Maybe you can help me figure out if I'm fit to continue the work, I love doing. I let someone down and it can't be fixed. I don't know if I can trust my own judgment. Being able to rely on myself, and knowing others could trust me has always made me a better cop."

It seemed like hours, instead of just fifty minutes. Finally, it was over. Out on the street the sun was brighter than ever, and his headache rebelled at the brightness. Putting on sunglasses didn't help much. Maybe, a nap before the Al-Anon meeting would help. When Andy got home, he laid down, but just tossed and turned. At least the medicine for the headache worked. Looks like long sleep days won't be needed anymore.

Faith Church was on Oak Place, a wide street with lots of oak trees down the center, with a double wide lane on both sides of the street for cars to go either direction. The center was wide and a block long, so Andy thought the residents must play football out there. There wasn't any street parking, but the beautiful church had a good-sized parking lot. It was an older building, but very well maintained. Several cars were there already. Andy arrived early, not wanting to be late, and come in after the activities had started.

He decided he had better go inside. To stay in the car wasn't an option. He opened the door and got out. Jean Baughman pulled into the space next to him. It was a good surprise to see her, and he said, "Hello, Jean."

She looked over the top of her car and smiled. "Hi Andy, hasn't this been a beautiful day? I hope I got all the dirt out from under my fingernails, I've been planting several roses. Are you here for the Al-Anon meeting?"

"Yes, it's my first time, what about you?" he asked.

"Yes, come on in and get registered. We can have some goodies and coffee. I baked chocolate chip cookies and my special recipe brownies. Hope you will love them," Jean said.

"Let me carry those," Andy said.

"Only, if you promise they will get into the recreation hall before you start on them," she said playfully.

He walked beside her, it was a comfort and disturbed him all at once. He had talked at work with her, it was easy, but this closeness was different and excited him. Those little hints of pleasure, and the desire to touch her had sparked between them. Was it only one way, or did she feel it too? If she was affected, she appeared cool about it. Not any sign of the tension that was there all around them.

When they got inside Jean introduced him to the people, who were already there. It was nice to have someone to smooth the way, Jean explained. "We eat as soon as we get registered, because many of our people are coming directly from work and haven't eaten anything since lunch. It's hard to concentrate on the meeting, if you are hungry." Then they got plates with a cookie, and brownie each, and coffee. The cookies were exceptionally good, but the brownies melted in your mouth, and made you almost cry for more. Jean caught the heavenly pleading look and went and brought them each another brownie. Handing him one she said, "I'm glad you like my cooking so much. Maybe you should come over for dinner one night when you're off. I have been told my pot roast is divine, by several people including preachers."

The meeting got started, and the dreaded spot of having to stand, tell your name, and answering, who was the alcoholic in your life? *Andy didn't want to do it. But that's the reason for being here tonight.*

"My name is Jean Baughman. My deceased husband was an alcoholic. I have been attending for four years, and I'm still trying to reclaim my own life." She sat back down.

"I'm Andrew Palmer, first time here. My father was an alcoholic," He sat down pretty hard in the low chair.

About thirty people were in attendance. Lots of stories about pain, mental and physical abuse. People struggled to cope with others drinking, and the effect on their lives. Some were almost traumatized; others were getting better using the offered tools to cope. It was a lot to take in, the teachings seemed so foreign.

Signs around the room said:

Distance Yourself. It's not all about you.

Don't take the harsh words inside you, let them fall by the wayside.

Andy wondered, how do you do that with a father who is standing over his son, telling him how dumb he is, over and over? Even thinking about it all these years later, Andy felt like that small boy. Luckily, he didn't beat you or anyone else. The hurt and pain was still there. Shutting off these feelings was his way to cope, but it must not have worked, or he wouldn't have identified that old drunk, with his own father, and made the worst mistake of his life. After years of being told he. "Would never amount to anything," he showed him! He's a goodcop, and better detective. He's somebody! At least he was until a few days ago, when he let down little Dana.

The meeting went on. Alcoholism is a disease. DIS-EASE. Everyone around them is uneasy! Watch out, he *almost said that out loud. That's not what they are teaching here.*

Think of the alcoholic like a person with a cold. Feelings wouldn't be hurt, if a person had a cold, and couldn't go out at the last minute. Look at the harsh words, as being part of the disease/cold symptoms, and don't be hurt by the insults and lies, or other unacceptable behaviors. Detach from the problems created by the alcoholic. Don't create a crisis, or take part in a crisis, started by someone else. Be an individual, and don't make excuses for the alcoholic or take the blame for their problems. Concentrate on self, instead of giving in and staying home from events to take care of that person. Take responsibility and let them take responsibility for themselves.

Andy wondered. *How could he have let his father get away with making him feel like it was his fault, Dad drank?*

The meeting was over and the participants started to leave. Many came to shake hands and invite him back. The preacher, Bill James invited him to church Sunday. And told him he would see him for the regular Thursday meeting too.

"I heard Brother James invite you to church Sunday. If you can attend, you can come home with me, and have that dinner I mentioned earlier," Jean said.

"Sure, that would be great!" Andy said.

"Will you be here Thursday night? I'm making zucchini bread, and peach cobbler," she said.

"If I come to these meetings, I may get rid of my anxieties, but become downright fat," he said laughing.

"It's good to have someone to laugh with, let's do more of this." she replied. Andy walked her to the went home feeling better than he had in years. At home, sitting in his favorite chair, was a pleasure, again. But the joy was marred by the knowledge of his part in the death of Dana Morrow. Would those feelings always be so close to the surface? He needed to tell Jean what happened the night he didn't send out the amber alert, and about little Dana's death.

Life sure has some strange twists. He'd wanted to date Jean for a couple of years, but never got the chance to ask her out. If he had asked, she would probably have turned him down. Yet, now that they have common ground with the Al-Anon meetings, she had asked him to dinner. Home cooked pot roast. He could almost taste it right now. His mother, and his deceased wife were the only one who had made a meal just for him. The women he dated, all wanted to go to fancy restaurants or fast food, no one had offered to make him a meal.

His mother had tried to make special meals for his father, but nothing was ever right for him. When he asked what she had done that day, she told him. She had done many praiseworthy things, but he would ask why she hadn't done something else too. His father made everyone around him feel like a loser.

Andy couldn't see how she had taken his abuse so long. But he now understood why she had refused the chemo treatments. She didn't want to stay around and keep getting her self-esteem pulled out from under her, and have her feelings hurt constantly.

Mental abuse wasn't talked about until years later. Distancing, like Al-Anon teaches, was unheard of at that time. His Mother had finally distanced herself, by allowing death to take her with no fight.

Andy was glad he had been able to leave, and never have the desire, to be a drinker. He had been happy his father hadn't been a part of his life for many years. Now, because of his feelings about his father he had allowed his judgement to be compromised, and let it interfere with his job. And now, Dana Morrow was dead. The amber alert might not have made a difference, but he would never know if it might have been a life saver. Andy might never be able to distance himself from the tragedy of little Dana's death that he had caused.

CHAPTER 4

Andy needed to sleep, but he found himself pacing
all through the house trying to work off the
agitation building in his heart over that terrified,
beautiful little Dana. "Oh, God forgive me!" His
anguished cry went up. We have all been told, God
can forgive anything, even murder.

His mind said he believed it, but his heart wasn't
sure. The desire to be forgiven is there, but
somehow, the tendency to hang onto the problem
stays strong inside. He believed God created
the world out of nothing, by speaking it into
existence. He trusted God's word that he will take
care of him. Is this trust issue because he feels
unworthy of forgiveness? Is it shoving away
God's hand when the trust isn't total? It seems too
easy to say, God this little girl's death is his
fault, but then ask your forgiveness, and go on his

merry way?

This is so overwhelming that he decided to go to sleep. He hoped sleep would come to him quickly. Maybe, it will be clearer tomorrow. He felt the depression as it set in. Perhaps, it's always an underlying substance, waiting for the right triggers to pop it out, and make a person aware it's there again. Or are we always depressed and just don't know about it. With a smile maybe, someone could pass for not down in the dumps. If he could fool others maybe, it would work for him too.

Andy tossed and turned awhile then remembered an old woman named Mrs. Blackburn, who always made him smile when he was a young boy. She sat on her porch in a nice chair with a shawl draped over it. Most days she would ask him to sit on the porch step by her feet. She didn't pry, but ask about school, family, and his plans for the future. She would sometimes tell him about her travels. She always seemed to be happy, and he always left her house with a smile on his face, and a lighter heart.

Now he wondered, if she really was happy all the time. Maybe, she was never marred by bad things happening in her life or maybe, she had already overcome them. Was she putting on a show for the outside world? He'd never been suspicious of her happy nature; just thought she was a sweet old lady that enjoyed life.

Thinking about Mrs. Blackburn did lighten his mood and he was finally able to sleep.

When Andrew awoke, he saw that it was another beautiful day, the sun is shining, and a bird is singing nearby. The coffee smells so good, wafting down the hallway. After a fitful night of tossing, it's time to get up. He couldn't keep turning off the alarm. Get up, dress, and go somewhere. Where? What does a person do on Wednesday? Ladies do lunch and card parties, talk on the phone, shop by themselves or ingroups, and read romance novels. What do men do? Maybe, handball or gym workouts, golf could be a big one? That didn't appeal to him.

Go to the mall, for new shoes, pants, and a shirt for Sunday. That's a good idea. Shopping is tiring. How do women just adore shopping? Lunch at the Chinese Palace in the food court, in the mall, tasted good. That was a surprise. The theatre, just across from the food area, has a movie he hadn't seen. That will take up some time. The kid, that sold him his ticket, looked like he should be in school. Andy bought some popcorn with heavy butter and a soda, a must for action movies. Maybe, the lunch should have been after the movie. There's an odd feeling sitting in an almost empty theatre. A couple of young people, an older couple, and a few others interspersed throughout the large expanse of tiered, comfortable, burgundy seats. Movie houses, usually, have neat carpet and chandeliers, too. This one is nice. Jean might like this one, if they ever got to the movies. What kind of pictures does she like? Probably chick flicks, he could sit through one of those. He would let her choose which one, she wants to see.

The movie started. Sound effects come up loud and draws attention directly to the action. Losing himself in a story is good. Another movie was starting in the next movie theatre when the first one finished, so he paid to see it as well. He couldn't stand sitting through a third one, so he decided to go home. He would stop and get some fast food at a drive-thru first. So many choices, he could eat a hamburger, Mexican food, chicken, ribs, Chinese food, or sandwiches. Never knew there were so many drive-thru places, one on every corner, and wall-to-wall down the street. Andy decided to go to Pizza Hut, for a pizza and sit down awhile.

He went home. Andy lived on a quiet street in a nice older one-story, yellow brick house with black trim. It was easy to maintain. The living area is open to the large kitchen with four baths and four large bedrooms. The man that built it wanted four master bedrooms, so he put two on each end of the house. Andy had been told Mr. Arnold the builder was afraid his in-laws would end up living with them. They each had their own bedroom, so he made one for the mother-in-law and one for the father-in-law at the far end of the house. They each had their own bathroom. He and his wife shared one bedroom at the other end of the house and, had a guest bedroom in case they invited company to stay over.

Andy had been happy here and guessed the house was a little big for one person. But it never seemed that way. What is going to happen with his job? What can he do about the situation, he created? The doubt and indecision are almost paralyzing. It's about three weeks until he can go back to work. Then what? With no one trusting him, maybe he should turn in his badge, and find another line of work. He felt like he was being stressed beyond his limits, slowly stuck in a fog, where it seems to have no way out, and no comfort to be had.

How in the world can Little Dana Morrow's, mother cope with her terrible loss?

Andy knew he had to stop this pity stream now! He couldn't let go of the life he'd built up and fall into despair. He had to go on. He can't quit. Even though, that seems the easy way, but he couldn't allow himself to slip away from his responsibility! Sleep! Maybe the Al-Anon meeting, tomorrow night will offer more coping skills. He sure needed something. Do they have any answers?

Up after another restless night, today he wasn't going to sit around and waste time. He had to get dressed and go out. The gym is an upscale place, that has all the most up-to-date equipment. Andy liked it here because it didn't smell bad like most gyms. The work out made him tired, he showered and dressed.

Then went to the gun range and did the regular monthly practice. All his scores were still good. On to the dry cleaners to pick up the clothes, he'd never liked to iron those shirts and pants. It was much easier to have them done. Another trip to the grocery store was needed. The day was going pretty fast. After lunch, he picked up a couple of movies. He was surprised to find himself wanting to see Jean at the Thursday night Al-Anon Meeting. He was thinking about her a lot these days.

He couldn't believe how much he looked forward to the meeting. Probably because Jean will be there, with her special homemade desserts. He guessed eating them wouldn't hurt anything, since that long workout this morning. Jean has been having strange effects on him.

He heated up the left-over pizza and ate. Then dressed in the new clothes he'd bought, black pants and light blue shirt. It's time to go.

As he turned into the parking lot he saw, Jean had just parked, and he pulled in beside her. She smiled and got out of her car and opened the back door. He arrived just in time to carry the food.

"Hi, great day," Andy said.

"Yes," Jean said, "had to work a little overtime this morning, so I didn't see the sunrise. Planted some more rose bushes, I have a super yard. You will get to see it Sunday." Several people were already there and introducing themselves to him again.

"Remembering names is a real challenge," a woman named Dorothy told him. "Some people talk to me regularly at the grocery store, and other places, and I can never remember who they are. I told my son, when he recently visited that if I was talking to someone, please don't be offended if I don't introduce you, it's because I forgot their name."

My son said, "I should just say I forgot their name, and ask what it is?"

Dorothy said, "That's hard to do, when I know all about their children, and when they had surgery. I have talked to them for over twenty years. So, since I know I haven't known you very long, is it ok if I just ask your name every time I see you?"

"Yes, that will be fine. I'm Andy Palmer. Please

excuse me a minute"

"Sure," she said.

Andy looked for Jean, he spotted her talking to a couple by the back wall. Observing her awhile before going over, he noticed the nicely cut dress suit in teal blue with a stylish longer skirt. She made it look good like a magazine photo. Conclusion, she's a classy lady. She turned and invited him over, then introduced him to Diane and Ellis Hamilton.

"Hi, we just got back from vacation in Hawaii. Have you ever been there? Retirement is nice." Ellis was enthusiastic.

"No, but you look like the sun was good for you," Andy said.

"Put it on your to do list, young man. It was wonderful, and the food was good. Those Hawaiian people sure know how to roast that pig, in the ground pit. We didn't like the Poi, but some of the tour people loved it. I think that was because it was new to them, and they had to find a new best thing. Diane chose Macadamia Nut Ice Cream, as her favorite food, she had to have a cone of it every day while we were there. I hope we can find it here." Ellis said.

"It's delicious. I loved the trip around the island in a boat. We saw a Grotto and the orchids and flowers were magnificent. One of the flowers blooms for three days only and it changes color each day. Then it's gone like day lilies, but the colors were outstanding. We went to the volcano; it was steaming, and orchids were already growing on the recently cooled lava rock. The Memorial and the

Cemetery are both incredibly sad. It was strange to see our soldiers and older Americans standing there and Japanese men right there, too. It was a trip of a lifetime, I'm glad we were able to go." Diane said.

The preacher, Bill James asked everyone to take their places when all were seated and quiet, he asked them to tell their name and why they were here. They went around the circle. A little imp inside Andy wanted to say, *"I came here to see Jean Baughman!"* Luckily, common sense prevailed, and he said what was supposed to come out. After names and introductions, a speaker was introduced as, Captain Bradley Johnson, of the Metropolitan Police Department.

It surprised his socks off. He looked at Jean and she whispered real low, "He speaks every few months."

He walked slowly from the back, turned and smiled then greeted them. "Hello, it's a beautiful night. Thanks for inviting me again. Each of you has been adversely affected by alcohol. I speak quarterly so some of you don't know me, since you're new to these meetings. My uncle Jim was an alcoholic. He beat his family, and one night came home drunk and shot them all. Then himself, with a gun he had purchased illegally on the street. This tragedy affected my life and I found help in meetings just like this one.

Some drunks are mean, others are nice and seem very controlled. With mean drinkers you need to get out of their way. Leave them alone. I do not care how much you think you love them. Get out if you're being hit or verbally abused. In my job I see mostly the nasty drunks. Most battered men or women when asked, 'why did you stay in that situation?' Will tell you, I love him or her, he or she needs me. Also, he or she was always sorry for hurting me and even cried and ask my forgiveness and I thought they would change, thought that they wouldn't hurt me again, or I didn't have any place to go."

In this day and age with shelters available we are still hearing the same excuses. Most of the time our loved ones think and really believe they are not hurting anyone but themselves. And tell you that over and over and some of them say you should just let them do what they want, and you live your own life.

But we have no control when we tell them to go their own way and we will do what we want because. What we want is to change them and make them into our idea of who they should be. The alcoholic wants to be the one to control you.

So, you're all going around in circles. The Twelve Step Programs have been around since the nineteen-fifties. They have been there this long because they work, helping to break the cycles of abuse. The alcoholic gets the benefit of no more drinking or drunken stupors.

They gain back self-esteem that has been lost. They get better health, and a better life. The people around them get their own life back, too. Each one finds they must depend on themselves and then they can help others. Once the anger is neutralized and forgiveness comes into play, life can take on a meaningful existence that brings the joy, peace, and harmony back into relationships.

I know last week you worked on detachment. Accepting that alcoholism is a disease and not getting angry when the symptoms arose to steal your peace of mind. We know that this takes a lot of practice and remember that's why each of you has a sponsor. Call them just to talk if that's what you need. They volunteered to help you because someone was there to help them. If you're not sure how to handle a certain situation, call and ask. God is there to help you always. Prayer is a great comfort. When you're not sure your prayers are being heard, and, those times do arise, call your sponsor. Attend meetings often, it helps knowing we are surrounded by others going through some of the same struggles. As you have probably already found out they want to help you make it out into the sunshine, where happiness is possible. Thank You."

Captain Bradley Johnson received applause, and Pastor Bill adjourned the Al-Anon meeting.

"Hi Andy, you looked like you would fall out of your chair when I was introduced."

"Yes, Brad, it was quite a shock to see you up there. I had no idea about your family. That's tough."

"That's why you were not fired on the spot, after your incident. The Commissioner also understands how hard it is to keep things in control. So here you're, learning better coping skills and to release the anger and frustration and guilt, we hope. Have you called your sponsor yet? Who is it?" Brad asked.

"Peter Duncan, he called me yesterday and we

talked awhile. Seems nice and he was able to answer some questions, I had," Andy said.

"Good, let me know if I can help. Glad Jean excused herself and went to get her belongings when I came up. She doesn't know what happened." Brad told him.

"Brad, is anything happening with the case? Has Bob been able to find out anything?"

"Just that the van was reported stolen from the airport long term parking lot when the owner got back from vacation. The ticket was in the cup holder, and they drove it through the ticket booth and paid on April 18th. Three days before the child was taken on April 21st. The van has not been found. The mother Mrs. Morrow reported the missing girl Dana Morrow hours later, on the morning of April 22nd. She worked a late shift and sometimes left the girl home alone. So, no one knew she was missing until the mother got home. Mrs. Morrow was real shaken up that ten-year old, Dana was missing and really devastated when the child was found, and she realized what had been done to her. The idea of delicate little Dana being beaten and raped and tossed away like trash in a dumpster is really disturbing to her. All of her family members were dead and so was the girl's father and he didn't have any living relatives either. She thought working hard was better than staying home and getting welfare. I'm not sure Mrs. Morrow, can handle this mentally. I got her some free counseling with a group that deals with the loss of a child. I hope it helps. In our job, we see a lot of mothers that could care less about their children, but for one that loves so much, to lose hers like this is worse. Andy, I'm not dumping guilt on you. You did ask me about what was happening. God will forgive us but it's the hardest to forgive ourselves. But it must be done for us to move forward into the future. Especially in our career path with so many people depending on us. You can do it, Andy. You believe that don't you?" Brad asked.

"Sure, I guess. Sometimes it's more positive than others. If not, maybe I could find another line of work instead of being a detective which I love." Andy answered.

"That's always an option; there are many service jobs where good men are needed too. But you have been too good a cop for us to lose you. I'm risking my own career so that you can come back with a vengeance to see justice done for everyone. We are keeping you in our prayers, too." Brad said.

"Thanks, Brad. Looks like Jean is ready, and I will help carry out the leftover dessert."

"Ok, but don't count on leftovers, when I got my zucchini bread not much was left. Take care of yourself. Goodnight." Brad shook hands and went out the door.

Jean was ready with her empty cobbler pan and a plate that had held zucchini bread. She handed a plastic wrap piece of zucchini bread to him and said, "I saved this for you?"

"He took it eagerly and thanked her." He walked her to her car and said, "Good-night Jean see you Sunday morning."

"See you Sunday." she got in her car and Andy watched her drive out of the parking lot.

When he arrived home, he turned on the television, then turned it off and decided to read a good book instead of television. Tommy Boyce, at work had recommended a series of five books by C.L. Wilson, a fantasy world she had created in the Tairen Soul Series. Andy had bought them all, at the mall the other day. It might be nice to go into someone else's world for a while. After the first few pages, he knew it was the escape that was needed right now.

CHAPTER 5

He was so involved in the reading that the phone ringing hadn't penetrated his mind. The machine had started its speech when he answered and said, "I'm on the line, hello?"

"Thank God, your home. I need your help, it's an emergency." Jean excitedly said, "Come by and pick me up as soon as you can get here. I live at, 1772 Sheridan Way. It's about four or five blocks from you. Dorothy needs our help. I will explain on the way. Please hurry. I will be outside." She hung up before he could say anything.

Glad he hadn't changed clothes when he got home, Andy slipped on his holster and gun, and put on his sport jacket over the top. Got out his keys and started off. Her house was easy to find, and she was standing outside as promised. She ran to the car and opened the door and got in before he could think about getting out to open the door for her.

"Dorothy lives at 954 Ambary Drive. It's about fifteen blocks from here. Go to the end of the street and turn left. Her husband came home and beat her up. She needs us to get her out, but she was not sure where he went or if he is still around the yard or gone. She didn't want to call the police and is very afraid. You look puzzled, what?"

"Which one is Dorothy?" he asked.

"Tonight, I heard her ask you if she could ask your name each time she sees you," Jean said.

"Ok, the nice lady in the pink pant set. She mentioned a son, does he know about her being abused?" Andy asked.

"Yes, that's Dorothy Hill. No, her son doesn't know. This is a second marriage and the husband and son never hit it off. Her first marriage was a good one, but her husband died a few years ago. Then she thought she had met the man of her dreams. That turned out to be a nightmare. She and Charles have been married a couple of years. He treated her good when they we're dating. The abuse started about eight or nine months ago. Then it was just harsh words and control issues then advanced to pushing. It was building with time. The total shock came when he broke her arm, by twisting it back at an odd angle. That was probably two and a half months ago. Women her age think, because that's what they have been taught, to stay no matter what, and you must do whatever has to be done in order to make your marriage work. If it doesn't work, you must have done something to cause him to hit you. It makes me so mad to hear those things," Jean said.

"And that makes the policeman's job even harder. Everyone always hated domestic calls. The officer tries to help them, but they might both turn on him, sometimes he'd end up dead," Andy said.

"Turn right at the next stop sign and go another block and turn right again. The house is about the middle of the block on the north side." In the small amount of car light Jean looked a little scared. Then she said, "You never know what will happen in a situation like this. Thanks for being here. Hope you're only needed for moral support."

"Glad to help out. I will be ready for whatever we find," Andy said.

Andy slowly drove past the house and looked around the area. Not seeing anyone, he went back and parked next door to Dorothy's house. It was a big, beautiful house with lots of flowers and huge trees.

Andy said "Use your cell phone and call her. See if it's clear to come into the house and if she needs help coming out. Does she know your voice on the phone?" at her nod, he continued. "Do you have the same Avon lady?"

"Yes, how do you know about that?" she turned to look at him fully.

Smiling, he answered. "They have territories, and she lives close enough to you. When you call announce yourself as the Avon lady."

Jean dialed the number, and the phone rang a couple of times before it was answered.

"Hello Dorothy, this is Alice Chapin, your Avon lady. Sorry to call so late but we just got that new promotion I was telling you about." She waited.

"Jean, he must be gone. I think something is broken I haven't been able to get up. There's a front door key under the frog in the flowerpot to the left of the door. I'm in the dining room." Dorothy said weakly.

"Ok, be right there!" she said and hung up the phone.

"Jean, as a dispatcher did your training teach you the room clearing procedure for entering, where a suspect might be armed and dangerous?" Andy asked.

"Yes, but I've never had to use it before," she said.

"Ok, follow me and stay back. I know you want to rush right to Dorothy, but we must check out everything first. I must know you won't be in danger of me shooting you in the process," Andy said.

"Good, got it, I don't want to get shot. I will stay behind you," she said, "Let's go."

They got out of the car as quietly as possible and left the doors not totally shut, just pushed up to the frame. Stealth was the motto as they crossed the yard and looked at everything and everywhere to make sure they were alone. The porch light was on as usual, but they would have to go up and get the key and enter.

Andy went to the planter for the key. It must not have been used for a long time and the plant had grown over it, making it hard to locate the frog and get the key out. Andy opened the door and pushed it quietly open and looked around before going inside.

There was plenty of light inside to see well into

the beautiful entry hall with a big chandelier. They entered and took a few steps. Waited and looked over the area then moved forward. Inch by inch they covered the house, and it was clear. Dorothy was in the floor almost hidden by the large dining table and twelve chairs. When they got up close, they both tried to cover their horror at her appearance.

Andy did a quick check of Dorothy's injuries and told Jean to get the tablecloth off the table and hand it to him. He used it to put pressure on the gash in Dorothy's side. It looked like a knife wound. A lot of blood had been lost. He tried not to move her any more than necessary. But he turned her, so the tablecloth and the floor put enough pressure to stop the bleeding. Jean calledthe dispatcher and told her the situation and ask her to send police and ambulance to the scene.

Jean spent the time before the paramedics came, gently holding one of Dorothy's battered hands quietly talking to her, as the injured woman continued to cry out of almost sealed closed eyelids. She was badly hurt this time. How many times like this had there been?

Dispatch connected Andy to Bob's desk. "Hi, Bob this is Andy, I need you to put out a pickup on Charles Hill. He got drunk and beat his wife, we're not sure how it will come out. Ambulance is on the way to the house. She looks bad, a lot of blood loss. No idea what he used to hit her. You might want to declare the house a crime scene just in case."

"Thanks for the information, Andy. How are you and how did you get mixed up with another drunk incident?" Bob asked.

"Dorothy Hill the victim goes to the Al-Anon meeting I attended tonight. I guess her husband didn't like that. Brad talked to our group about leaving if you were getting hit or had verbal abuse. She can't talk right now. So, we don't know too much yet. I'm doing ok I guess but this makes me want to be able to prosecute this guy."

Bob said, "That's better than wanting to beat him to death."

"I thought of that but decided I was a lawman instead of executioner." was the comeback.

Bob and Andy talked like normal. Maybe that's a good start back to the cop he had been. He sure hoped so. Why does it take an ambulance so long to get here? Jean seems to be holding it together, even though there is a lot of stress in her facial features. How could it be otherwise seeing her friend in such an awful condition.

Bob said, "Officers are on their way to the scene, and we'll look for Charles Hill."

Andy stepped back into the room with the ladies and saw Dorothy was moaning a bit from the pain she couldn't control. Jean was still giving reassurance and quiet prayer. That seemed to soothe them both. Maybe prayer did do some good.

Andy saw his hands and phone were covered with Dorothy's blood. Some had been wiped off on the tablecloth. Jean had blood on her hands too. He felt like he was paralyzed as he stared at his hands. First little Dana and now sweet Dorothy, so much violence and too much blood.

"I hear the ambulance so I will open the door for them." Andy called over his shoulder, as he already moved quickly. The attendants asked the usual questions: what happened, how did it happen, how long ago, name, and age? As one was writing all this down the other two went into the house to check on Dorothy.

When Andy and the third man came in, they already had put a pressure bandage on the knife wound and had taken her blood pressure and put an oxygen lead on her. The leader was doing a broken bone search to check her condition before trying to move her. He said, "Get a neck brace and we will put the immobilization splints on both legs and the left arm, before we can transport her."

After that was done, they lifted her onto the gurney. The carpet was soaked with a large pool of blood that was turning that ugly brownish color.

The emergency room doctor was on the phone with one of the paramedics telling them how much of this or that to give her and transport immediately. The paramedic was repeating for his partners, what the doctor told him.

"Ok, ready to transport!" They started for the door, pushing the gurney carrying a pitiful looking Dorothy, with IV bags hanging from a short pole on the gurney.

"Can I ride in the ambulance with her?" Jean asked.

"No, you can meet us at Mercy Hospital Emergency Room. Are you family?" one of them asked her.

"She is a good friend. I will follow you there as soon as I can," Jean said.

As they got to the door two policemen were

there. One was Bob Simon.

"Can I talk to her, a minute?" Bob asked the paramedic leading up the team.

"Sorry, Bob, we need to transport, now." the implied urgency was not lost on any of them. Bob moved aside so they could pass.

One of the paramedics leaned back in the door and gave Andy a plastic bag with a roll of paper towels and two bottles of water. He said, "You and Jean might want to step out and clean the blood off your hands. If this is a crime scene as it looks like you don't want to use the bathroom." He ran to the ambulance, and they were gone.

Andy and Jean took advantage of the towels and water to get the blood off their hands. Jean noted that her outfit was ruined. The stains would never come out but if didn't matter all she could worry about now was Dorothy. Andy put the debris back into the plastic bag.

"At least the reporters haven't arrived," Andy said to Bob.

Bob gave a weary nod, "They will be right behind us, do you know this guy?"

Andy told him as the two officers entered and he shut the door. "I don't know them. I talked to the wife a couple of times," Andy said.

Bob said, "Hi Jean, sorry not to speak sooner. Are you ok? Is she a friend of yours?"

"Yes, I have known her several years. I will have to change clothes before going to the emergency room. I hadn't noticed my clothes until I got up from the floor to wash the blood off my hands, this outfit's ruined."

"Can you sit down here and tell me about her and her husband?" Bob asked helping her into a high back chair.

"My husband and I met them at church when she and her first husband attended. They were a lovely couple. We took turns hosting and had lots of fun game nights when we would play Mexican Train Dominoes, or card games like Canasta. Four years ago, Vick died. She was so lonely. A good marriage leaves you feeling like part of you is missing when one dies. Her son David Benton lives in Seattle. So, she was all alone. No other family living."

"Charles Hill started attending church services. I think it was about the time I lost my husband Don to cancer. So that would be just over three years ago. He was nice and everyone thought he was a good person, kind, and helpful. Apparently, he is a good architect. Most of the new buildings on the south side of town are his designs. He was recently interviewed in that famous architect's magazine.

He acted like he was falling for Dorothy right away. She put him off awhile, but he was persistent. They dated a few months then one Sunday he announced in the church service that, "Dorothy and I are getting married and everyone is invited to the wedding. Date to be announced." he smugly smiled at everyone.

Dorothy was surprised. She later told me, "It was a total shock, he hadn't even asked me first. Just put it out there in front of all our friends. He apologized and told me he just thought I loved him as much as he loved me and was moved to invite them to our wedding. It sounded romantic. He loved me that much. She thought it was a good sign," Jean said.

Shaking her head Jean added, Dorothy said "When the verbal abuse started, he was under a lot of pressure with his work, so she just attributed it to that. The mean words continued. Dorothy, tried to discuss the problem with him and he told her, he didn't have any problems. She was just too dumb to know that it was her own fault."

Jean was getting angry telling the story, but she was holding onto control. "I don't know when the shoving started, then a few slaps, then worse. About two and a half months ago she came to church with her left arm in a cast. When I asked her, what happened she looked scared and told me she fell and broke it. I was not convinced, and she knew but didn't change what had been said."

Charles said, "She's getting clumsy with old age."

"I was surprised to hear his derogatory comment, and more convinced than ever he had done this to her." Tuesday was the first Al-Anon meeting she attended. I didn't know she was going to be there. Then two days later, tonight, she attended again. That may be what triggered this attack. That's all I can tell you, Bob. I hope they find him soon," Jean said.

We left Jean in the living room while we did a thorough walk-through of the house.

Bob observed, "The attack must have happened here in the kitchen and after he was gone, she must have gotten to the dining room before collapsing. Good thing she was able to grab the phone. The drawer is open that holds utensils. I would say he had been hitting her and then, probably got out a knife and slashed at her with it. It doesn't seem to be here so he must have taken it with him when he left."

The other detective, Paul, was writing everything down in his notebook. As he had Jean's statement.

Bob mentioned that The other detectives that had been dispatched were checking the grounds.

As we opened the back door, one of the officers came over. "Hi Bob, Andy, we found a kitchen knife over by a tree close to the alley. We think someone dropped it and got into a car out there. Looks like a blood trail from this porch. The techs will have to bring their equipment to make sure. How is the lady? The television vans are out in front. We have been keeping them off the property."

"Thanks, Joey. Good job. We don't know anything, but Dorothy looked bad and John Markham, the paramedic was in a big hurry to get her to the ER Doctor." Bob said.

"I play cards with John; if he was in a hurry, it must be urgent." Joey replied.

Back in the living room Jean was praying. When they entered, she finished and asked, "What do you know this far?"

"I'll tell you in a little while. I called a cab to meet us around the corner. We will walk down the back alley and go to Ash Drive, leaving my car here. The alley has already been cleared. The media are all out front. The cab will take us to your house, so you can change, and we can take your car over to the hospital. Is that ok with you?" Andy asked.

"Yes. I saw the media swarm, from the window.

Lucky this chair sits back far enough I don't think they saw me. One of them started for the house but an alert patrolman headed him off," she said as she rose from the chair and tested her foot to make sure she was standing steadily. Noticing his look, self-consciously she added, "Sitting too long sometimes makes the arthritis act up a bit," Jean said.

"Is walking bad for you? We can leave another way if it's too much," he said.

"No, walking is good for it. Getting up is the hard part. Once I'm standing solidly, I can usually walk ok. Let's go," Jean said.

We said goodbye to Bob and went out and made sure not to step in any blood spots.

Walking down the alley with her would have been very pleasant, if we weren't both wondering how Dorothy was and what was going on? We hurried in case the taxicab got there quickly. It was not there, but the wait was not exceedingly long. Andy opened the door of the Green and White Cab Company car and handed her in, then followed. He gave the driver Jean's address.

CHAPTER 6

Jean's home was lovely. It suited her. It was white wood with deep garden green trim, with lots of roses, and many different flowers. She asked him to sit in the living room while she changed clothes.

Looking around at the nice furnishings, he saw a lot of feminine touches, but it wasn't a room that a man wouldn't enjoy relaxing in too. Large masculine chairs were sitting in front of the fireplace, with a nice sized table between them. Lots of room for a snack dish and coffee cup on each side. A set of lion bookends, holding several recent books, and several cozy mysteries. He owned several of the same ones. It's nice to know someone else who likes to read.

Jean entered the room with a tray with coffee and snacks and placed it on the big ottoman. "Let's have something to eat before braving the hospital. I made coffee and tuna sandwiches and got out the chips."

He took the plate she offered and the cup of steaming coffee. "This is really thoughtful for you to do this."

"That was part of my childhood lessons, be a good hostess, besides, I was hungry. Hospital food is on my list of never do again unless absolutely necessary." she laughed.

What a nice sound, her laughter rings in his soul. Watch out, she is winning him over. Maybe she already had.

"What did you add to make such good tuna salad, was it small pieces of grape in there?"

"You got it," she said.

She is glowing in this light. "It's delicious, thank you," Andy said.

"I have pecan pie. Would you like a slice?" she asked.

"Yes, I would."

She took our sandwich plates and returned with two pieces of pie. Then poured more coffee before sitting down again.

"Did your husband like to read? This is a perfect place for reading a good book. And I noticed a lot of varied books in the beautiful bookcase by the wall and here on this table."

"He did like to read. We liked many of the same ones." she remembered with a slight smile.

Andy thought. *I hate to question her, but I need to know and this is possibly the best time to find out, so do it.*

"Did your husband ever hit you?" Andy asked.

She hadn't expected that and was taken aback by

it. Then said, "No, he was a melancholy person when he had been drinking too much. His personality was even tempered most of the time. So, it was hard to tell until he said something about his childhood and got to feeling sorry about it. Then I knew. I felt I had to be his protector and not let anything hurt him. I only went out of the house for short periods of time, especially when he retired and was here all the time."

"I went to my job and got along well there in that environment. When I got home I went into protective mode. He had heart problems, cancer, and other illness that we dealt with until he died. That went on for about five years. After he died, I didn't know how to handle it. Brad called me into his office one day and we talked a long time. When he found out that my husband drank, I saw the light bulb above his head flash on and he said, "I have just the thing for you, Al-Anon! You will love it. That's where you will learn to control your own life again. You are a nurturer and so you gave too much of yourself away. Come to the Tuesday meeting at our church. I'm the speaker. You won't be going into a group with people you don't know." Brad said.

"That's when I started and I'm getting myself back to whole again." she smiled. "Did your father hit you?"

He should have expected that one, his turn. "Not hitting, but his hard words felt like you had been punched. Nothing you or anyone did was right. He made you feel guilty, like it was your fault that he drank. You ask him to stop drinking and he said,

"'I'm not hurting anyone but myself. Just like Brad said tonight."

His cell phone rang, it was Bob. Excusing himself he answered. "Hi Bob, what is going on?"

"Just wanted you to know, Charles Hill came home with clean clothes and asked, "'Where is Dorothy?'" Real drunk still according to the breathalyzer, but he is lucid enough to have changed his clothes somewhere. My bet is he had extra clothes in the car he drove away and dumped the bloody ones before coming back. He is acting mighty innocent and wants to go see his wife at the hospital. He wants to know what we are doing to find the people who entered his house and did this to his wife. With all the audacity of a big shot, who is very offended that we would think he might have done wrong to his wife. How is she doing?"

"We don't know yet." I muttered. Not wanting to let him know I had been engrossed in other matters and we hadn't even gotten to the ER.

"Are you still at the house?" Andy asked Bob.

"Yes, we will be taking him into the station soon. He got a chance at the press before we got to him. They have his innocent sounding inquiries about his wife on tape, as he arrived home to find chaos. Keep me posted when you hear more on the wife, ok."

"Sure, Bob," Andy said.

"What is happening?" Jean asked.

"Turn on the television, let's see what Charles Hill had to say to the press." Andy told her.

"Ok, come this way, tv's in the den." she turned it on. We sat down to watch. There he was driving up to his house. The driveway was blocked by the television vans. Reporters rushed the car. "Sir, who are you? Are you a friend of the family?" The reporters asked.

"What is going on here what are you all doing in front of my house? What has happened?" Charles asked.

"One of the women reporters ask him, "Sir, you mean, you haven't heard what happened to your wife? Have you spoken to the police yet? Where have you been?"

"No, n- n- no what happened?" Charles stuttered.

"Your wife has been removed from the house and sent to Mercy Hospital. She has been beaten. You don't know anything about it?" The pretty blond shoved the microphone into his face again.

"Oh, Lord. I must get to the hospital. Who did this?" he whined.

Just then Bob interrupted and led Charles into the house. Detective Bob Simon took him to the kitchen through the dining room where blood stained the carpet, then led him to a chair to set down.

"Mr. Hill, where have you been?" Bob started the interrogation.

"Some bar, I don't remember where." He hesitated.

"How long were you there?"

"How do I know, a long time, I guess. What happened here? Are you searching for the criminals who did this to Dorothy? When can we go to the hospital to find out about my wife?" he answered angrily.

"Did you hurt your wife, Charles?" Bob asked.

"Of course not!" he shouted outraged.

"She told us you did." Bob said.

"What, how did she tell you anything?" Then realizing what he said he backed off and added, "She's crazy you know! She doesn't know what is happening most of the time. Someone came in off the street and did this terrible thing. I have a right to go and see her." Charles ranted.

"So, you thought you had killed her, did you?" Bob stated.

"What are you talking about? I didn't do anything!" he screamed. "You're wasting my time here when my dear wife is in the hospital. Accusing me, instead of looking for the real culprit. I want my lawyer, NOW!"

Bob looked at him and said, "Calm down, you can call your lawyer when we get to the station." Then Bob read the Miranda rights to him.

"Paul, we are ready to go." Bob told the officer who wrote down all that had been said. Paul wrote, that down too, and timed it. They could take these notes into a court and hopefully get this man put behind bars.

Bob said, "Charles, come on."

Charles Hill tried to talk to the press gathered outside but he came across badly and the police car moved out with him in handcuffs in the back seat.

After watching the news coverage Jean said, "Coming out he didn't come across on tv as smooth as when he went in looking innocent. Wow, he sure looked crazy by calling everyone names and shouting and being so angry. Probably makes all who saw the broadcast want to convict him right now. He was attacking those around him too."

"The lawyer will probably use it to claim he is crazy and can't go to jail. We had better get to the hospital and check on Dorothy," Andy said.

CHAPTER 7

Jean said, "Big hospitals make me queasy. I hate the smells, disinfectant, medicine, and sickness. I read somewhere that diseases have different smells, too. And that dogs can tell if a person has cancer. Maybe they can pick up the scent of illnesses."

"What was that?" Andy asked. He had missed what Jean had said.

Jean continued, "It's ironic, but I think this hospital is a building that was designed by Charles Hill, a few years ago."

"They need moving sidewalks in hospitals. The halls are the longest ever. Hard to visit on a short timetable, with miles to walk to get to the persons room," Andy said.

At the ER reception desk Jean asked, "Where is Dorothy Hill?" Thinking she would still be here.

The young girl looked at her screen and said, "I

don't have her listed."

"She was brought in by ambulance a little over an hour ago." Jean told her.

"Not listed here. Let me call back, just a minute." she turned away and spoke into the phone. She swiveled back and announced. "Sorry, we can't help you."

"Miss, I'm Detective Andrew Palmer. I need to know about Dorothy Hill," he said showing her his badge.

She quickly got on the phone again. Then turned around and told him. "You'll have to go to the surgery waiting room on the third floor. The doctor will talk to you when they finish with her surgery. Go down this hall to the back bank of elevators. On the third floor go right and down to the reception desk and turn right again. You'll see the sign."

He smiled and thanked her. They went down the hall and found the elevators. We got to the subdued peach color waiting room with comfortable chairs in a blue gray design. Bill the preacher was there.

"Hi, Jean, Andy, glad you came." Bill said, "The doctor told me, Dorothy may not make it out of surgery, but they will do all they can for her. He will come out when the surgery is done and give us more information. I gave them the information on her son David. I'll need to check to see if they have reached him." He looked apologetic as he continued, "Do you mind if I go down and get some coffee and donuts? I missed dinner tonight, so I ate some of Jean's sweets at the meeting but I'm getting hungry. I didn't want to go down while I was the only one here but since you came, I think I should do that."

"Do go, Bill. We'll hold down the fort." Andy assured him.

Bill took their hands in his and said a prayer for Dorothy before he took his leave and as he was going out the door, said, "I'll bring back coffee and chips, ok?

"Sure," murmured Jean.

She had looked so stricken when he had told them Dorothy might not make it. Andy wanted to take her in his arms but knew it was not proper. *Better to take things slow with her and not frighten her away, by pushing their growing friendship too fast.* They sat, not talking much while they waited. He saw that she was praying a couple of times. She looked so tired. That's what this waiting and stress will do to you. He noticed she kept looking at him often. *That's a good sign, isn't it? Maybe she would like his arm around her shoulders. How is a guy supposed to know?*

Bill returned with good coffee and tortilla chips and guacamole dip. He sat it down on a table and said, "come and share with me. I went to the gas station that I always liked their coffee and got some food. Hope you like these."

"I think I could live on guacamole dip. I did for a time once and never got tired of it." Andy told them. "I'm surprised to be hungry again."

"Love it." was Jean's reply.

"Then it's good that I got the big giant bag of chips." Bill said and smiled.

When everyone was settled and had a plate of chips and dip, Bill asks, "Has there been any news?"

"No, we have just been waiting." Andy told him.

"I stopped at the desk on my way back and ask about them reaching Dorothy's son David and they had just gotten him on the phone. He told them he would get the first flight and rent a car at the airport. It will probably take several hours." Bill said.

Jean looked stricken, she said, "I didn't have his phone number with me. I should have had it."

Bill assured her "The hospital has it on their records, so it's not necessary for you to worry about it."

"I heard on the news that Charles has been arrested, do they really think he did this to her?" he asked.

"Oh, Bill, he did. She told me on the phone. I called Andy to go with me and we called the ambulance. Lucky she could call, or she would have died for sure. She could hardly talk when we got there. It was awful. How did you get here before we did?" Jean asked.

"I usually have the scanner on with all police calls and ambulance. I was in the car driving when it came on and I called the ambulance dispatcher, Evelyn, and she told me they were going to transport her to Mercy. Clergy has a few privileges if you want to call it that. It usually helps the family if you come when they or a loved one is in an emergency. I saw them bring her in and then talked to John the paramedic. He told me she didn't have much chance. Too many things going on inside her body. I hate to have one of my own congregation members involved in something so unsavory. And losing one is always hard for me. I have been praying for her to live, but if she does, that she can have a meaningful life. To live and be injured to where life loses its joy, isn't what she would want. We discussed this once shortly after her first husband died. She wants to be healthy, but if not that, then to still be active."

Doctor Kaplan Greene entered and looked at them. Are you all here for Dorothy Hill?

"Yes." We all said as one.

"I'm Doctor Greene. Dorothy made it through the surgery and is now in recovery. It will be quite a while before she comes out of the anesthesia. We'll keep her under as long as it's safe to do so. Both legs were broken. The left arm is broken, again. Our records show she had broken it not long ago. There was a lot of bleeding from the knife wound to her side. Nothing vital was severed. But she will have a nasty scar. She was beaten savagely. We won't know the extent of the damage done until she can talk again. There could be brain damage. We'll watch her closely and do all we can to make her as comfortable as possible and hope for the best. Please leave your phone numbers with the desk out here and we will call you if there are any changes. When she comes out of the drug induced coma, she will be taken to the Surgery ICU so the nurses can monitor her and be right there with her. We have taken the precaution to take her name out of our system. I understand the reporters are hanging out in the hospital and trying to get any information they can. That's about all I can tell you right now. Please go home. If she comes out of this, she'll need her family and friends to be rested and able to help her. Any questions for me?" the doctor asked.

Jean asked, "If she makes it out of the coma you have her in, how well would she be able to function if there is no brain damage?"

"I would expect her to be in the hospital for a long time. She would have to heal a great deal before starting therapy. The one leg was broken in three different places. She'll need both physical and emotional therapy after such a trauma. She may never be the person you knew again. Anything else?" he asked.

Andy said, "Doctor I would like to talk to you outside."

"OK, that will be fine," he said.

"Bill, nice to see you here, wish it was under better circumstances." The doctor left them.

Andy walked out with him into the hall. "Doctor Greene, I'm Detective Andrew Palmer, Metropolitan Police." he flashed his badge. "Did she say anything to help us get the person who did this to her?"

"I was just headed to call the police. She became alert for a short time before we started the anesthesia. She said her husband had followed her to church and was mad because she went there and told her he was going to kill her. Detective Palmer, it's on our surgery room tape. For insurance we tape everything now." Dr. Greene told him.

"Do you know what he was hitting her with?" Andy asked.

"I don't think she knows. There was mention of being hit extremely hard then when she woke up there was blood on her and everything hurt. She found the cell phone and called someone."

"How soon can we get the tape?" Andy asked.

"It will take a few minutes. I will have to call the administrator. She will contact the technical support guy to make a copy for you. You'll probably need a warrant so she can turn it over to you." Dr. Greene said.

"Ok, I'll wait, be right back." Andy told him.

"The nurse here will guide you to my spot to crash for a little while, See you in a few minutes."

Andy went back to Bill and Jean. "Bill, will you make sure Jean gets home safely. I have to stay and do some work." Andy told him.

"Thank you for coming when I called, and for getting me through tonight. See you Sunday," Jean said. Then she hugged him gently.

Pastor Bill said, "Me too, see you Sunday. Goodnight."

They left him there and he pulled out the cell phone and called Bob. When he answered Andy said, "Good, glad you're still there I need someone for chain of evidence, we may need a quick warrant for a tape made during the surgery of Dorothy Hill. She named her husband as her attacker."

"Ok I will be there right away. Danny will get the warrant for me. Tell me where to go once I get in the hospital." he waited for Andy's directions.

"Ok, got it. See you soon and thanks a lot. Nice work." Bob said.

Andy went to find Doctor Greene.

The nurse at the desk was writing on a chart as Andy came up to her.

"Hi, Detective Palmer, Dr. Greene just talked to us and told me to let you know where to find him. Go down that hall; turn right, he is in the second office on the right," she said very pleasantly.

He pushed the door open. Dr. Greene was on the cell phone. He waved Andy in and motioned for him to sit down.

Hanging up, the doctor said, "The hospital administrator, told me we will need a warrant to give you the copy of the video tape. But the tech, Pete will make a copy for you."

"No problem, my partner, Bob Simon, is on his way and is getting the paperwork we need. He is working this case and will handle the chain of evidence. We want everything done by the book." Andy told him.

"If you don't mind, I'm going to lie down over by the wall and sleep awhile. The television won't bother me if you want to watch or there is a bookshelf over here. The ADMIN will call me when they have your tape ready. Don't worry I'm a light sleeper. The coffee there was just made for me a few minutes ago, help yourself." he went to the couch and stretched out.

It was a large couch, but he still didn't fit all the way. But he looked like he was in a comfortable position.

Andy went right to the books. Found one he had read about half of at his house and picked up the story where he had left off. This lounge was made for comfort. With his high-backed tall wingchair and cup of coffee he was ready to take his mind off the events of the last few hours.

The surgery took hours and Dr. Greene had said three of their surgeons worked on Dorothy. *How in the world do doctors do the long hours and only get catnaps like now?* They never know what new emergency will be next. Thank God there are people willing to do that job, it sure wouldn't be for Andy. The hours he put in are long and hard sometimes, but the doctor's job is worse.

CHAPTER 8

Bob slipped through the door and came over to Andy. It had been about forty-five minutes since Andy had called him. They talked quietly, hoping not to wake the doctor until the call came in that the tape was ready for them. It was another forty-five minutes until the phone rang.

"Doctor Greene," he answered.

They both looked at him and were surprised at how fast he was alert and taking them down the hall, to the administrator's office.

"How do you guys walk these long halls daily? It would kill me, Bob complained.

Dr. Greene laughed. "I wore a pedometer a short time and averaged eighteen miles a day. I decided I really didn't want to know. I must sign some papers for the ADMIN on why I requested the video for you. Here we are." he opened the door for them.

"This is Nancy Anderson, our hospital administrator." He introduced her.

"Nancy this is Detective Andrew Palmer and Detective Bob Simon." They all shook hands.

Nancy an attractive brunette, invited them to sit down. Then said, "I need a warrant to turn over the video to you."

Bob opened his folder and produced the document they needed and handed it to her.

"Thank you." She looked it over and added, "I went to school with Judge Alice Dixon, her last name was Lawrence then. Pete is on his way with the video tape. Would any of you like some coffee while we wait for him?"

All declined the offer.

Andy decided this would be a good time to put in his two cents on the long walks to get anywhere in a hospital. They all smiled at his idea of a moving sidewalk in the halls. It was mentioned that some hospitals had tram systems that took elderly and infirm people where they needed to go. The conversation continued until Pete arrived.

He tapped lightly on the door and opened it, walked in. "Do you want me to set it up so you can watch it?" He asked.

Nancy said, "Yes, please. When it's ready you can leave."

"Ok, ma'am." he set it up to show on one of the little individual sets they use to show patients what kind of procedures they are going to have done. "Ready, press this button." He left. They watched Dorothy being rolled into the surgery room and the preparations that were still being made. The anesthesia Doctor Bryan Alban, nurses Susie Dean, Josie Johnson, Andrea Porter, and Callie Bright entered the room. Doctor Kaplan Greene pointed them out. The orderlies that had wheeled the patient in had left. Dorothy had been moaning, but it was getting louder now. Then she opened her eyes just as Doctors Kaplan Greene, Phillip Donne, and Paul Kelly arranged themselves around her. They looked her over to see where to start, what needed the first attention.

She started talking loud enough to come through on the tape very well.

"He said, he was going to kill me! He hit me," Dorothy said.

Doctor Greene, leaned close and ask her, "Who tried to kill you?"

"My husband followed me to church and back. Mad, at me. Hit me! Hit me! I woke up and I think he was gone. Red all over me, everything hurts so bad, phone in pocket. Jean talked. I have to sleep." The medications were working on her.

Dr. Greene said, "That was all of it, for Dorothy."

They had the whole operation on tape and that would be for the lawyers to deal with. Bob signed for the tape, and we left the hospital.

As we were leaving, Bob said, "He thought he had killed her before he left. When I talked to him, I told him she told us he had done it, and he said, "'How could she tell you anything?'" He realized his slip-up and clamed-up and asked for his lawyer. With all this evidence we should be able to see him go away for a long time."

"Bob, thanks for everything, I owe you a big apology for not following up on that old drunk guy Perkins. I'm sorry I didn't listen to you. I will never forget that little girl Dana Morrow. Can you forgive me?"

"In time, right now I'm still trying to track those two young men. I know you checked for missing children that day and on stolen vehicles. Neither had been reported yet. Do you think the Al-Anon program will help you?" he asked.

"I hope so; I didn't realize how angry I was at my father after all these years. Guess it has been building up a long time. They are telling us to detach ourselves and try to see the alcoholic as someone with a cold. That's hard to take. But if someone had the cold and was genuinely sick, you wouldn't get angry when they weren't there to do something you wanted them to do. So instead of trying to fix them you should concentrate on yourself."

"Good luck with it and come back soon. I must get this tape turned in and go home. Bye now." Bob headed for his car and a taxi was waiting for Andy.

Green and White Cab Company was getting a lot of his money lately. Twenty-six dollars to get to where he'd parked his car just down from Dorothy's house. He got out and paid the driver. Charles Hill's car was parked crookedly in the driveway from where he had been blocked by a television van in his way when he arrived home. Andy went to it and saw a parking garage ticket in it.

Did his car get checked before they all left the scene? It was locked. Andy pulled his phone out of his pocket and dialed. *Cell phones seem to automatically appear in one's hand these days.* "Bob, did you just get to the office?" Andy asked.

"Yah, it takes time to drive that far. I got the tape logged in to evidence." Bob replied.

"My car was here at the Hill house. Was Charles Hill's car checked before we left? Did they check for blood with the blue light? *Yes, I know it has a big, long name, but blue light is what it is, and it shows up blood.* Good, there is a parking garage ticket showing in the seat. It looks like a ticket from that place over by the Southside Mall. I wondered if he had rented a car and followed her around, parked in the alley and then picked up his car and came home. That would explain, no blood on his car or clothes. He could have gone somewhere and changed too. A nearby motel maybe, if so, he planned to kill her," Andy said.

"I will pass this on to next shift and get them working on it. Good job, Andy. I goofed not getting his car brought in tonight, we'll fix that. Oh, Charles has been held without bail. Seems his lawyer liked his wife better than him and refused to defend him. He will have to get a public defender, or he will probably call another lawyer when he gets the chance. Bye." Bob said.

CHAPTER 9

When Andy got in his car he started home, it was kind of anticlimactic. Maybe a couple of cardboard waffles in the toaster would be good and a glass of cranberry juice. Then sleep all day. He slept until about 8 P.M. Friday night. Andy got up made a sandwich and drank a glass of milk. He hoped his next-door neighbor Mrs. Frankel would send over more of that rye bread with the caraway seeds on it. It had a strong flavor not like the rye you get at the store. He read a couple of hours and went back to bed and slept well the rest of the night.

Saturday morning was bright and sunny. He needed to do some yard work. It was a good day for it. He fixed oatmeal, with strawberries and milk and a cup of yogurt. Ate it and then washed the dishes and went outside. His small garden was good at growing weeds. He had to pull them and pick some fresh vegetables, for a salad. His mind wondered as he did the chores he enjoyed.

If Andy had put out an Amber Alert, that night, what would have happened? "An Amber Alert has been issued at 4:41 P.M. Be on the alert for young parochial schoolgirl, wearing a burgundy plaid school uniform. Reportedly abducted by two men in a van, that was gray, or silver color with a sliding side door. Partial plate A--44-. One of the men had dark hair and the other had an odd blue color in his hair. If you see this child or the van don't approach. Contact the local authorities immediately. The public is asked to help us apprehend these suspects by information given to us of any suspicious sightings. Thank you. Repeat..." Would anyone have seen them or known these men? Would we have found her before anything bad had happened to her, more than the fright of being pulled into the van? Andy would never know. He couldn't change the decision that allowed her murderers more time to do the awful things she must have endured. If he had been on target that night, what else could have been done to catch those two? The phone was ringing when he entered the back door with the fresh vegetables.

"Hello," he said.

"Hi, this is Jean."

He was smiling; her voice was so welcome in his ear.

"Bill just called. Dorothy is not doing well. Would you mind coming over for lunch? I don't want to be alone, and I can't see Dorothy at the hospital. I know you're a busy man and it's asking a lot but it's all I could think of doing." her voice trailed off.

"Sure," he said brightly. "If you will let me bring the salad, I just picked fresh vegetables from my garden. I have some ham and cheese should I bring that too?"

"Great, I was going to give you tuna again. I do have home baked light bread, sour dough bread, and pecan shortbread cookies, made this morning!" Jean said.

"Sounds like a feast to me. Is an hour ok? I have been weeding and need to clean up a bit before anyone can see me for all the dirt." Andy told her.

"Good, I will be looking forward to it. Bye." she hung up.

Singing on the way to the shower he wondered, *how can she do that? Make everything seem alright by inviting him over. Wow, she has gotten to him big time! If she knew how he'd failed little Dana, she would never want to talk to him again! How could he stop the self-recriminations when it's justified?*

Andy thought he should call Jean and tell her he can't come over. But she is counting on him to help her get through the possible loss of a good friend. *Would the biggest disservice to her be by drawing back or going and maybe getting in deeper with her than he already felt they were now? Had he ever been this indecisive? Is it part of his grief over what happened to Dana? Does grief make you want to crawl into bed with the covers over your head and sleep away the rest of your life? And makes it hard to function in your regular daily chores and duties?*

Ok, enough. He gave his word. He must go, if only to get himself out of the house. But he knew he wanted to see her. *Is that being selfish, to spend time with her just to be close to her? Especially when he knew he's not the type of man she really needs?*

In this light her house looked bigger, and the landscaping was magnificent. It was laid out by colors. Here all red flowers over there by a tree were blues and purples. Then rose only beds and rose and wildflowers together.

He must ask her to walk around the yard with him. He rang the doorbell and waited for her to answer. She was wearing a sapphire blue pant set with a blue and white print blouse, that softened the shock of the bright color. It suited her perfectly.

"You look beautiful, maybe we should go out to some fancy place for lunch," he said as he handed her the bowl with the vegetables and ham and cheese.

"Don't be silly, I just got back from the hospital. They wouldn't let me see Dorothy or even tell me how she was doing. They act like they never heard of her. I know Dr. Greene said they would do that but thought since I was there last night, they would make an exception, I guess. Life is confusing right now. Follow me to the kitchen and we can start fixing the food."

The table was set for a party with cups and saucers instead of the mugs they used last night. A nice floral centerpiece not built up too high in the middle so people could visit over it, sat on a lovely damask tablecloth of creamy white made it look festive.

"Do you want to cut the bread or the vegetables?" she asked, glancing at him.

"Veggies, I might eat the loaf of bread before it got cut. May I please have sourdough?" His mouth was watering. "And the end crust of the light bread with butter for dessert?" he said.

"Ok, then we can take a stroll around the rose garden and later have cookies and coffee," she said.

Lunch was very pleasant, good food and conversation.

Jean said, "Let me tell you about my roses. I have them grouped in special beds. I always loved roses. One day my husband brought home a Bing Crosby rose and a Frank Sinatra. We started adding to the collection. Singers in one rose bed. Movie stars like Ingrid Bergman, Katherine Hepburn, etc. in another and so forth. Audrey Hepburn had to go in another place, so she was with her contemporary stars like Grace Kelly.

I think that my Eleanor Roosevelt was probably the first in the political collection. We bought those copper markers and imprinted each with the rose name so we would remember. The Pope and some saints are over there next to the water fountain." she pointed. "Across in the bed beside them are the royals. Then almost in the center is a big section for the David Austin Old Style cupped roses, like you see in the famous old paintings. Most of the antique roses are usually climbers, they are all around the perimeter of the yard."

He had made the appropriate comments as she pointed all this out and enjoyed the stroll.

"You really love this garden; it shows when you talk about each one and tell about their color and fragrances. I noticed you had flowers interspersed with your herb garden, but you don't have a regular vegetable garden. Why don't you grow your own vegetables?" he asked her.

Jean gave a hearty laugh. "Donald, my husband said, "'I don't like vegetables and don't want to grow them. Herbs and lettuce ok, maybe a tomato or two but that's all!'" So, we put in the herb garden without vegetables." She smiled, and continued, "Years and years of work and love are represented here. History is all over this yard, of movie stars, singers, politicians, people and interesting colors and scents are bountiful for months at a time.

Jean said, "They bring joy to lots of people. I have a wonderful group of ladies who help me with what I call the flower ministry. During the blooming season they usually come over for Tuesday luncheon here. We do a potluck. Everyone brings a dish. They each have their own specialty. Ellie never cooks so she brings chip and dips. Gina bakes a cake and decorates them like magazine photos. Andrea makes a potato dish she must have a cookbook with one-hundred-one recipes for potatoes. Jean giggled. Patty takes care of salads. Donna brings meatloaf or roast or a chicken dish. I provide the bread and cookies, coffee and tea, plates, and silverware. We have good food and wonderful company."

She continued, "After lunch we go out and cut the roses and put them in buckets with water to keep them fresh over-night. As we cut them one of the ladies strips off the thorns and another puts a little tag with the rose name on it. Wednesdays we take them to the two nursing homes here. We try to make sure each person has a beautiful rose.

People love to know they got, a Peggy Lee rose today or Princess Diana or whoever, they usually know about the celebrity. And most of them have stories to tell about a favorite star. Some always want the same one. When we know that we try to see that they get it. The men like the reds mostly such as Mr. Lincoln, Chrysler Imperial, Memorial Day, Veteran's Honor and Oklahoma. My bud vases are left there and we add the new rose. If the one from last week still looks good, we will leave it and add a new one. If it looks worn, we change it. You always use fresh water and a little crushed aspirin to make them last longer."

"Impressive, I'm amazed that you do all of that for others. How long has this been going on around here?" he asked completely awed, by her kindness and thoughtfulness.

She looked thoughtful then said, "Almost ten years. We enjoy doing it so much and feel blessed each time we do it. Some of those people have no one left to remember them and everyone loves a thing of beauty that belongs to them."

Jean said, "One of the ladies at Summerfield Nursing Home, Judith Roberts, saw us bring them in the first time and saw that we had many colored vases. I told her to choose the first one. She asked if one of the deep reds was named, Ingrid Bergman and it was, so she chose that one. Mrs. Roberts told me she had been sent three of the rose bushes when they first came out, by Miss Bergman, herself. Judith had been an extra in one of her movies and they had become friends."

Andy said, "Wow, that gives the residents of the homes something to talk about. You must have lots of good stories like that one, that have been passed along to you."

"Yes, one lady, Edna, loved flowers, so one day the nursing home had a big yellow mum plant given to them. It was placed in the lounge where everyone who entered the building would see it. Edna picked herself a bouquet and took them to her room and put them into a pitcher that held her water. The nurses were shocked when they saw the plant with hardly any flowers left, until they found them in her room. She lived in her own little world and didn't realize she had done anything wrong. So, no one mentioned it. She told people, "'look at the beautiful flowers growing in my yard.'" She has been gone several years now. I planted a mum at her grave."

Jean looks incredible in this light. The sun has moved and it's not as bright as when they started walking. Andy thought. *He would like to enjoy times like this with her the rest of his life. Where did that come from? The rest of his life, was he thinking marriage? She would settle for nothing less. Jean would never marry him if she knew his dark secret. Could he live without telling her about Dana, the abducted child, and his part in her death? If she found out later, she would hate him for sure. Better just enjoy this time he had now and not get any closer to her.*

"What was that?" he questioned.

"I asked, if you were ready for coffee and dessert." Jean said.

"Yes, that will be great." Andy smiled. He did that a lot when he was with Jean.

He saw that they were at the back door, and they entered. She didn't forget the request for light bread and butter, there were also cookies on his plate.

Jean is so thoughtful, what a neat person. A great woman, who doesn't need him. *How sad, to finally find the one who makes his skin tingle and makes him hot just looking at her.* Before the child Dana, he would have been confident in pursuing her. He decided he must get going home soon.

Andy said, "I'll call the hospital to see if we can get any information on Dorothy. This is Detective Andrew Palmer; can you give me information on Dorothy Hill? She did? Oh, thanks. I will," he said then hung up.

He turned back to face, Jean. She looked frightened. "She took a turn for the worst during the night but is doing a little better right now, but it could go either way. They have no way of telling. It just goes from patient to patient. Will you be alright if I go now? I don't want to leave if you still need some comfort."

"I have to confess, I just wanted you to come over today. I will be fine. You will come for dinner after church tomorrow?" She asked as her face showed a beautiful red tinge.

"Yes, I'm looking forward to it. Thanks for a great day today!"

At the door she leaned close, and he could smell her perfume and shampoo and something else mingled together. He wanted to grab her and give her a kiss filled with desire. Instead, he took her hand and kissed it lightly. It was like an electric shock. *How could kissing a hand do that to him? Did she even notice. He felt hot and bothered and she looks cool as a cucumber. Did he really use that old saying even in his mind*? She did blush a bit when she invited him back tomorrow. Better get out of here quick.

Driving home was not what he wanted to do. He would like to stay with her every minute. *Had he ever felt this way about any woman before now*? He didn't remember the confusion and mixed signals. When he courted his wife Melanie, everything went as planned. Life was easy with her. He'd loved her and thought he would die when she did. After a time, he started dating with no long-term plans with any of them. He knew what to do and how to act around them.

With Jean he got the idea she liked him as much as he was feeling for her. But the far away distant coolness was there also. Maybe she didn't want to give in to her feelings or perhaps it was it all his imagination. Right now, all she needed from him is a shoulder to help her with her distress over Dorothy.

She hadn't asked if he had been married. Most women ask that right away. They wanted to know everything about him. That's if they were interested. Maybe she knows his wife Melanie died six years ago. Cancer struck again! If so, that could be why she didn't ask. He thought he was falling in love with Jean Baughman. *What can he do about that? No way he could marry her without telling her about Dana Morrow the child he didn't save. That would probably end it. If she had any feelings for him that knowledge would turn into hatred.*

Andy knew he had to turn off his thinking, so he picked up a book he's been reading and sat down. Sitting in his favorite blue chair, reading this good story makes you forget where you're at for a while. The author makes up a total world and populates it with fantastic creatures and makes you care about them and what is going to happen next. How amazing is that?

Could you make up a colorful world like that and add your own language and words, no one thought of before now? Give your characters totally fabricated names and identities? Are authors born with that kind of imagination? Castles, dungeons, old caves and shacks, lush surroundings all colors for grass and trees and animals.

About 1:00 A.M. Andrew got to bed. Another fitful night, tossing and turning. Dreaming of Jean screaming that he'd killed that little girl by his negligence.

Dozens of cars in the church lot this morning, the walk will do him some good. Bill greeted him at the sanctuary door. "Heard anything new on Dorothy?" Andy asked.

"I called early; she is still about the same as yesterday afternoon. She had a bad turn but was doing slightly better then." The preacher said.

Entering the sanctuary, Andy saw the large pews, with blue cushions, and nice blue carpet. The pulpit was an old carved wooden piece, that was beautiful.

A master craftsman must have made it. The table for the communion and alter was a matching wood carved piece. Large paintings on the wall depicted the journey of Christ from Baby Jesus to Risen Lord.

He spotted Jean about halfway up the center aisle and joined her. She smiled a warm welcome. He told her about Dorothy's condition, and they talked until the service started. Bill James was a good preacher. His sermon today was on Paul, who had persecuted and put to death, many Christians. He was forgiven and was used as one of the greatest of Jesus' followers. Paul wrote several books of the Bible mostly letters to the new churches.

As they were filing out Jean whispered, in his ear. "I hope you don't mind, I invited Pastor Bill and his wife Georgia to lunch too. You will still come, please?"

"Yes, that's fine we'll have a lively conversation. I haven't met Georgia yet." Andy said. The dinner was delicious, and he enjoyed Georgia and Bill's company. They were a good couple. They all laughed. It was time to go, and he was reluctant.

CHAPTER 10

Bob Simon called, Monday about one-thirty to tell Andy that "Charles Hill has gotten a new lawyer. Noland Kenner, that high powered attorney with a big office and staff and they are trying to get him out on bail."

"Hope they don't get a judge to let him out. Are you going to the courthouse?" Andy asked. "Yes, I want you to meet me there, you can tell about Dorothy's condition when you found her." Bob said.

"Alright see you in about twenty minutes." Andy said

He was out the door and drove as fast as possible, he got there before Bob. They went inside together.

"This old courthouse was built when designs and beauty were part of architecture. I love these green and white marble floors. Look you can see a bit of gold striations in it, and some black and many shades of green. The big white columns make it look grand." Andy said.

Bob said, "Yes, it's always cool in here. It adds a bit of awe to the law procedure to me. My grandfather was a lawyer and used to tell me about an older man named Henry and a redheaded woman named Selma who were the elevator operators. He always had enjoyable encounters with them. He said Henry was good at predicting how long a trial would take. He and Henry would bet on it.

"Ah your, grandfather lived in the good old days. Another job eliminated by so called progress," Andy said, and they both laughed.

Bob said, "Here we are at room 404." They entered and the prosecutor spoke to them. The judge was announced and entered in her long black robes. Judge Jennifer Du Port, mid-fifties, decent looking, she had short brown hair and she looked very efficient. Her not quite stern-faced countenance added to her dignity. She had been elected to the bench for the third term this year.

When the officer brought Charles into the courtroom, he looked mean and harsh. Bob Simon was called as the arresting officer. He was sworn in and seated.

A well-dressed man stood and walked in front of him. "You rushed to judgment when you arrested Mr. Charles Hill on the night of his wife's alleged attack didn't you Officer Simon?" the attorney asked.

"No sir, Dorothy Hill said Charles Hill was the

culprit and she absolutely was severely injured and had definitely been attacked." Bob answered.

"Did you even look for any other suspects, other than Mr. Hill?" The lawyer asked.

"No sir, his wife said Mr. Hill was guilty." Bob said.

The fancy lawyer was not even phased by this. He just kept up the line of questions. "Did she tell you directly, that Charles Hill harmed her?" he asked Bob.

"No sir, she spoke to Jean Baughman on the phone and told her then. When Mrs. Baughman and Detective Andrew Palmer were in the house, she told them both." Bob stated.

"So, you arrested my client on hear-say evidence?" the lawyer said.

Bob smiled at that.

"You think it's funny that you arrested a man on faulty reasoning?" the attorney said.

"No sir, the correct man was arrested. No faulty reasoning involved." Bob said.

"That's your opinion, and since you didn't search for another assailant, you chose the easy way and arrested Mr. Hill instead of doing your assigned job didn't you?" Attorney Kenner asked rather smugly.

"No sir, Mr. Hill returned to the house almost two hours after our crime scene team arrived. We had done a thorough search of the house and grounds and had put out a pick-up order for Mr. Charles Hill. He arrived and we spoke with him until he realized he had incriminated himself. Then he asked for a lawyer, at which time the talk with him was over and he was arrested. His lawyer refused to represent him. A public defender was appointed by the court." Bob said.

With an, I got you look, the attorney continued. "So, you grilled my client until he broke then you seized the opportunity to arrest him, didn't you?"

"No sir. Mr. Hill, entered the house and started talking until, he asked for his lawyer." Bob said.

"I'm through with this witness, your Honor." Attorney Kenner said.

Bob stepped down and sat in the audience seats next to Andrew.

"Your Honor, my client was railroaded, and we request his immediate release. He has a house here and is not a flight risk as he is interested in finding the perpetrator of this crime against his beloved wife." The attorney said.

The Prosecuting Attorney, Eleanor Temple, a petite, thirty-something, well-groomed woman stated "Your Honor, Mr. Hill has no money of his own, due to huge gambling debts. The house belongs to his wife and since it's believed he committed this crime no bail should be granted. With no holdings he is a great flight risk to flee prosecution since there is a great possibility of his wife Dorothy's imminent demise. In that case the charge will be raised to murder instead of attempted murder. After Mrs. Hill's broken-arm a couple months ago, we believe her will was changed and Mr. Hill will receive nothing. She has a son we are sure would inherit all and the two men have strong feelings toward each other, so her son won't be disposed to share anything with Mr. Hill. We request that bail be denied."

This was news to Charles, and he jumped up red faced and shouted, "She can't do this to me! I went with her to make a will when we got married. She's not smart enough to change it without me."

The judge, got his attention by banging her gavel and said in a calm voice, "Mr. Hill, please sit down and keep quiet."

He slumped back in his seat and looked older, with his shoulders rounded and body leaning forward, dejected.

Mr. Kenner looked mad, he had thought the money belonged to Charles, or that he would inherit. Perhaps, that's what he had been told, on taking the case.

Judge Jennifer Du Port made her decree, "Bail is denied. Remand the prisoner to the Jenson Facility until his trial. Good day."

Mr. Hill was arguing with his attorney until the guards led him away.

Mr. Kenner hated to lose anything, and it showed. He hurriedly left.

Bob and Andy went over to shake hands with Mrs. Temple and congratulated her on this victory. Sometimes the good guys do win. Not often enough, though.

Bob and Andy went to lunch at Shirley's Diner. Reported to have, "THE BEST RIB EYE STEAKS IN THE WORLD!" At least that's how the big sign on top of the small building read. That sign was looking a bit worn these days.

"Hi, boys, how have you been? It has been a while since I have seen you. You haven't been eating steaks somewhere else, have you?" the waitress teased them.

"Josie how could you even suggest that?" Bob looked properly shocked.

"Hi, Josie, we've been working our fingers to the bone and couldn't get over here." Andy claimed.

"The usual?" she asked.

"Sure." they said as one.

Andy said, "It's good to see that some things never change." Josie and this place are an institution. No changes had been made. It was still clean, and the food smelled good.

They were laughing and enjoying the camaraderie that they had both missed the last few days.

Bob, stated. "It's good to be laughing with you again. I missed it. Let's stay on track from now on, ok?"

"That's what I want, Bob." was the grateful reply. "Anything new come in on the Dana Morrow case?"

"Not so far. Been tracking guys. One of them has blue in his hair, do you realize how many kids are doing that now? It's wash out colors, so today it could be electric blue and tomorrow orange or any other color they choose. The stolen van has not turned up so it may be out of state. The alert went out nationwide." Bob said.

"Josie arrived with the Rib Eye Specials, a big steak, baked potato loaded, salad and fresh sour dough rolls made on the premises with real butter. Large, iced tea was included. Bob and Andy smiled their appreciation.

Andy told Josie, "You always make the best iced tea. Very few places you eat out have really good tea."

"I would tell my mom thanks for teaching me, but she died years ago. Thanks for the complement." Josie said, moving on to another table.

Good conversation and kidding followed, and they both enjoyed the meal. Bob had to leave. He told Andy, "I'll keep you posted on the case. Glad to see that Charles will stay in jail awaiting trial."

The rest of the week went as usual with the visit to Dr. Breen, the Al-Anon meetings and household chores. Andy talked on the phone with Jean most evenings.

Saturday brought work, lawn mowing and gardening. Most of the day Andy spent daydreaming about Jean and he was looking forward to Sunday.

He sat with Jean in church. Then she suggested they go to the nearby park. She surprised him with a picnic lunch. Andy hadn't had such a great day since his wife had died.

CHAPTER 11

Housework and grocery shopping had filled the morning. Now it's Tuesday again time to go see the psychologist, the bland Dr. Breen, who seemed so out of place in his own office. They must send people to school to learn to ask questions and give no answers. If the patient is supposed to talk to a doctor with degrees and years of education, it seems they could tell them something and the doctors would have some answers for how to handle the problem. But they ask, "How, do you feel about that? Or "what would you do about that?" Oh well, perhaps Andy can get some insight into the anger problem.

"Hello, Mr. Palmer, please take a seat. The wait will be about five or ten minutes. Would you like a cup of coffee or tea?" greeted the receptionist, who fit her surroundings perfectly.

"Thank you, coffee would be good," Andy said.

She came around her desk and handed him a cup of coffee, after asking how he took the beverage.

He sipped the hot coffee and told her. "You make a very good cup of coffee."

"Glad you like it I get it from a missionary couple that started a business selling the area coffee, they hire many villagers. The money made from the coffee, is used to support their mission, and increase the local economy. If you're interested, I will write out the information, for you."

"That would be kind of you. Yes, I would like that. I have already thought of people who are on my gift list to share it with." Andy replied.

She said, "Doctor Breen is ready for you." as she handed him the information.

"Thank You. May I give you a compliment? You fit this elegant office setting beautifully," he said.

She blushed at the unexpected appreciation and smiled as he started down the hallway.

Andy said, "Hello Doctor Breen."

"Hello, detective please sit down. How are you today?"

"Angry."

"What are you angry about?"

"My drunk of a father!" Andy said.

"Was he always drunk?" Doctor Breen said.

"Most of my life, my mother said, it started when I was about five years old."

"What happened when he drank?"

"He ran my mother down; nothing she did was ever good enough for him! If I tried to protect her, he verbally attacked me, too!" Andy said.

"Was he always angry?" the doctor asked.

"Yes, no one could do anything that pleased him!" Andy said.

"Is he still abusing your mother?" the doctor asked.

"No, she died. She had cancer and refused chemo so she wouldn't be with him anymore."

"You blame your father for your mother's death?"

"Yes," Andy said.

"Do you still see him?"

"No," Andy said.

"Have you ever considered forgiving him?"

"NO!" Andy said.

"By not forgiving him, who is being hurt by it? You or him?" the doctor asked.

Silence invaded the room.

"Has your father ever asked you to forgive him?" the doctor asked.

"No."

"Has he contacted you since you left home?"

"No." He hesitated and said, "I take that back I got a letter a few years ago. But I didn't open it."

"Andy, do you still have the letter?"

"I threw it in a drawer. It may still be there." Andy answered.

"That's your assignment this week. I want you to find the letter and read it. Then take a piece of paper and put down what he wrote to you and how you feel about what he said. We'll go over those feelings next week. It's alright to be angry. What we want to do is defuse it and make a plan for dealing with that anger. The goal will be to find a way to redirect those feelings." he stood up and the men shook hands.

Now the anger is out in the open. *How can he defuse it? Read that old man's letter. I don't want to read it. Isn't that a childish thought?* He decided to take a nap before tonight's Al-Anon meeting.

But when he got home, he had too much energy to sleep. He went through several drawers looking for the letter from his father and found it.

Why did I keep it all these years? It was sealed and looked just like it had the day it arrived. Look at the cheap postage. The date stamp isn't very clear. *To open or not to open, not now!* He put it on top of the dresser in plain sight. He could read it later, maybe much later.

The plan for now is to take a book out under the tree and drink a tall glass of iced tea with a sprig of spearmint and a lemon slice.

This is the life drinking tea and reading, sitting in the comfortable lounge chair. He was so involved in his book that he skipped dinner. Since he hadn't changed clothes, he continued reading until it was time to leave for the Al-Anon meeting.

Driving to Faith Church all he could think about was that *Jean would be there. She sure has taken up a lot of my thinking time.* He smiled at himself in the side mirror. He arrived early and waited for her to get there. Several of the group came and waved or said "hi," then went inside. He waited. Then saw her turn into the driveway and park her car. He got out and went over and greeted her and took the pie and cookies to carry into the building.

As they walked in, she said, "Sorry to be late.

One of the flower ladies was sick today and we didn't finish as quickly as usual. We know we should add some others to help us out, but we are content with the old timers we have now. Maybe that's selfishness. Expanding our horizons may be a good thing to do, but if you invite the wrong person, they may not fit with the others in the group. Guess we should each start looking for compatible friends to add. Or maybe we are starting to feel the age creep up on us and want things to stay the same."

He opened the door and instead of the meeting in progress, people were standing around everywhere.

Bill said, "Hi, would you two open the dessert and serve it with the coffee Marion made?" He looked haggard. "At the last minute we found out our speaker wouldn't be here, and we can't get the projector to work. Angela is looking for a broom for some trick she wants to show us. You came in the nick of time to save the day!"

Andy joked. "Was that Mighty Mouse, that came to save the day or one of the other super-heroes?"

The apple pie was sliced and put onto the plastic plates with forks and the cookies displayed on the table. Someone else had brought pumpkin pie and it was plated, more plates held bite sized muffins, maybe two bites of cranberry or blueberry or banana nut and poppy seed. They brought enough of the bites for an army. But they were disappearing fast. The group started picking out their treats and filling their coffee cups. No one was complaining about things not working properly tonight. Small groups of two, three to five talked and laughed.

Angela brought her broom to the middle of the

room and told them to, "Watch this! TA- DAH!" She sat the broom with the broomstick in the middle standing straight, bristles going east to west she held it a minute and gently let it go. It stood there by itself. She again yelled, "TA- DAH!"

Amazement showed on the faces around her.

Then someone asked, "How did you do that?" Another asked, "Is there glue on the bottom?" Angela was laughing like a little mischievous girl. "I've been told this is a scientific phenomenon. You can do it at home with your own brooms. You're supposed to be able to stand an egg on end too. But I didn't want to clean up a broken egg in case it didn't work for me, so I didn't try that one. I have been having fun with the brooms, though. I heard about it on the internet and went to the big stores and lined brooms in the aisle and watched as customers walked by them and moved their cart around them. No one noticed anything unusual. How weird were they? When have you ever seen a broom standing alone?"

Before she could start again, Alvin said, "My vacuum stands upright by itself all the time." all present laughed at that.

"Oh," said Angela, laughing also. "Let me tell some more of my adventures. I went to my exercise group and set their broom in the center of the room where it had to be passed to get to the next machine. I told the workers not to say anything and see how long before anyone mentioned it. That was 8:30 A.M. and women moved around it until one woman came in at 10:00 A.M., looked at it a couple of minutes and ask, "How did you do that?"

"The owner said the lady thought this was a Halloween prank, since she and her co-worker wore wax lips and wax mustache for Halloween the week before when she came into exercise."

"Then I stood one broom up in the grocery store and was looking at it when a couple came by the end of the isle. They looked at it and I said, "'Neat, isn't it? A broom that can stand by itself."

The man looked at the broom then at his wife and nudged her and said, "If it will stand by itself, maybe you can ride it." His wife gave him a look. Angela knew he had said dumb things like this before now and wondered if he would get any dinner that night."

Angela continued. "This is fascinating. If the broom at home falls she stands it up again and it has stood a long time. Not sure how long it's supposed to last. The news reporter said that the planets are aligned exactly right now to make the magnetic effect that allows this to happen. She will continue watching it until the magic is gone. Weren't things simple and magic when people saw the man, in the moon, before astronauts went there. The man in the moon has no mystique anymore. Not so romantic."

Everyone agreed and clapped their hands in appreciation for her performance. Bill announced they had the film fixed and everyone could take their places and watch. It was about the steps to helping you find the way to your better life. ADMIT THE PROBLEM EXISTS.

They knew they had a problem. But hide it from others. Is that the thing to do?

Andy thought, *Who would want to tell others*

about their problems? Don't people avoid friends and relatives who always tell their business? His father has a drinking problem and Andy hated him for it! Hate really? Now it has become his problem, with the anger and frustration and a giant error in judgement with little Dana, with no way for that to be fixed.

The screen is showing, WRITE A LIST OF PROBLEMS AND SOLUTIONS.

If they knew the solutions, they would have already taken care of them. *Was he making this harder than it should be or is it hard to accomplish?* The film is over, and he missed most of it rebelling against the first two points in the list. He needed to take something for this headache and get some sleep. Maybe things will look better in the morning. He should check with Bob and find out about Dorothy. Pastor Bill mentioned he had been to the hospital today and she was about the same.

Andy didn't have headaches like this before that child Dana died because of his problems. Now he had more problems than ever.

Andy got a glass of water and took a couple of pills and hoped the headache would be gone by the time he got home. He walked Jean to her car and told her good night. Even with his pounding head his heart pounded like a hammer too. He stepped back reluctantly and let her drive away.

He fell into bed and slept well for the first night in a long time, with no nightmare or bad dreams. No tossing and turning, peaceful restful sleep, how refreshing to the human body. Amazing how the body can heal itself during sleep.

CHAPTER 12

Bill called, about 10:00 A.M. "Dorothy has taken a turn for the worse. Do you want to pick up Jean and bring her to the hospital? They will let her go in and see Dorothy."

"Does she know yet? Or do you want me to tell her?" Andy asked.

"I called; she is ready. She hoped you wouldn't mind bringing her up here. She didn't want to drive right now."

"Ok, I will be glad to pick her up. What did the doctor say about Dorothy's chances?" Andy inquired.

"Not good. He will be surprised if she makes it through the day. You might be here a long time. Is that alright?" Bill said.

"Sure. We'll do what needs to be done. I will call and let Jean know I'm on my way and see you in a few minutes. Bye." Andy hung up.

Her phone rang a long time, and she was kind of breathless as she answered. "Hello?"

"Jean, this is Andy. Just got off the phone with Bill. I will be more than happy to drive you to the hospital."

"Good, when he said he would ask you, I wasn't sure I should be so dependent on you. Do you have other things you needed to do today?" Jean asked.

"This is fine with me. If I can help you in any way, I want to do that. I'm on my way."

He was surprised to see all the cars in her driveway and around the street. Women loading buckets of flowers in their vehicles. Jean had told him about this, but it was a production in progress. A profusion of colors, this was as good as he had seen in parades. The ladies moved along at a quick pace. He asked if they needed help and was told that, "We have been doing this a long time and know what to put where, besides, Jean needs you to drive her to see that friend in the hospital. Thanks for the offer. Maybe you can join the group and help us another time." the white-haired, pretty faced one, told him.

He rang the bell and Jean appeared quickly with her purse in hand. She went over and spoke to her friends and bid them good-bye. They talked about the flowers for the nursing homes on the way to the hospital. They skipped lunch and came early to deliver today without me, so I could be with Dorothy. I may have to help her son make arrangements for Dorothy's funeral.

Once they got to the hospital, they had to walk a

good bit to the elevators and up to the sixth floor, it was farther to the surgery intensive care unit. The nurse said Jean could go into see Dorothy for only five minutes. And that he would have to sit in the waiting room. He knew what she would see when she walked into the area with all the medical equipment, some of the machines beeped and made strange noises. Dorothy looked unbelievably bad. She was not awake, and her black and blue arms and face were startling. Jean had heard patients could hear you even though they were in a coma, so she started talking to her softly about the love of Jesus. Praying that her words would be comforting to her friend. The nurse, Susan, told her it was time, and she could come back every hour for five minutes. She walked down a few doors to the visitor's waiting area. Bill and Andy were waiting for her.

Back and forth they went to visit, Dorothy.

Late evening the doctor told them all to go home. She had made an upward turn, but it was only prolonging the process and they needed to get some rest.

Reluctantly they decided to take the doctor's advice. Said their good-byes and Andy took Jean home. He didn't go in but said good night on the porch. She looked so tired.

When he got home, he found himself pacing around the living room and kitchen picking up newspapers and other articles that were out of place or he was just moving things around for something to do. He knew he would have to tell Jean about little Dana Morrow and his part in her death. He decided to tell her tomorrow night after the Al-Anon meeting. He was afraid she wouldn't be able to forgive him and not want to see him again. That would hurt but how could he expect others to forgive him when he wasn't able to forgive himself.

CHAPTER 13

After the Al-Anon meeting instead of telling Jean the truth about his guilt, he asked her out to the movies. She had eagerly agreed she would love to go to the movies. When he got home, he was restless.

Several of the group attendees tonight had talked about their experiences with the letter writing step.

Paloma, the young twenty-five-year-old Mexican girl, spoke about the letter of forgiveness she had written to her father, Jose and mother, Rosa. "My mother had been separated from my father more than a year. Mama worked at a small grocery store. She picked me and my brother Joey up from Grandmother's house one evening.

She took us to the small house she rented. Fed us and put us to bed. Patty, the neighbor's teenage girl, came over to stay with us while she went out with a friend Roberto.

The kiss Mama gave us that night was the last one from her.

Roberto and Mama got home and as they got out of his car about 11:15 P.M., Papa stepped out from behind the huge eucalyptus tree. He shot them both.

Neighbors heard the shots and called the police. Jose sat on the lawn next to mama until the police arrived. He was arrested right there and told the officers his story. Papa was sentenced to death for his crime.

I was about four years-old and my brother Joey was about two. We went to live with Grandma, mama's mother. We never saw Mama or Papa again, after that night, which as small children we didn't understand. Jose Rodriquez had been drunk at the time of the crime. Drinking was the cause of the marriage breakup.

A friend at work, Nelda recently steered me to Al-Anon, to help me deal with all those experiences. Denial and pain and other feelings were keeping me from becoming the person, I desired to be."

Paloma Maria Rodriquez read the first letter to her mother.

"Dear Mama,

You left us! We didn't know you couldn't help it. We thought you didn't want us anymore! Grandma Maria often took us to a big place with so much green grass and lots of stones, with all shapes and sizes.

Grandma said, "Your mama was laid to rest here. She is with Jesus." She cried when we ask her,

"'How did Mama get under the ground? When will she come home? Why did Mama leave us? How did Mama get from the dirt to Jesus?'" And many more questions.

Now I know, it was a lovely cemetery, where Grandma Maria was taking us, to visit your grave, the stone is beautiful. It's rose colored with heavy lettering and a rose etched on it. On the bottom is written: WE LOVE OUR ROSA.

I was so angry. Years went by and I never understood that you couldn't stop the result of that terrible night. You and Papa had been living apart for more than a year and he was not a problem until that night. Everyone was totally surprised!

Mama, I joined this Al-Anon group and I'm getting help dealing with the loss of both of you. I have missed you my whole life. My anger is gone, I understand that you didn't willingly leave us!

Your Loving Daughter,

Paloma Maria Rodriquez"

Much applause and well-wishing followed the tearful reading. Paloma was choked-up and asked Pastor Bill to read the one written to her father. Pastor Bill read the letter. "Dear Papa, I missed getting to sit on your shoulder at the parades. I decided not to go to parades after you were gone from us. I raised such a fuss and cried for Papa, I got a spanking. Grandma Maria never took us to a parade again. Joey didn't remember you. He only knew that we didn't have a mother or father anymore. We both felt abandoned. Grandma Maria was good to us and raised us to be good people.

That didn't make up for you being gone from us.

Through this Al-Anon program I have let go of my hurt that you left us and took Mama away. The letter is so I can put you in the past and go on with my life. You and Mama will always be in my heart, but I must not let your actions keep me from doing the things I need for myself. I love to draw and make clothes. I took design classes at the local Junior College and want to enter the world of High Fashion Design. Important people in the business have contacted me to work in an apprenticeship position. I called back today and accepted the job.

I must put you in the past where you and Mama belong, so I can move forward. I love you Papa!
Your Beautiful Daughter,
Paloma"

For those of you to whom I'm reading these letters, My Al-Anon Family, "'My Beautiful Daughter'" is what Papa always called me."

Everyone got up and hugged Paloma and congratulated her on her giant step forward and the new job. Not many were left dry eyed, it was a very moving experience.

"Paloma, you're a very brave and talented woman. I have seen those designs you showed us a few weeks ago. Continue to stay close to us and make a happy, profitable life for yourself." Jean told her.

Andy and Jean talked after the meeting, and he told her he'd pick her up at 7 P.M. tomorrow night for dinner at Anthony's and then the movie. They had decided on a chick flick, SEVENTEEN BOOKS AWAY. About a reading competition at the library with a special prize the young girl wanted to win.

Andy was tired and when he got home, he went to bed early. He slept better tonight.

The first thing he saw upon awaking Friday morning was the letter from his dad on top of the dresser. Maybe it was time for him to open it. He decided to shower and dress and have breakfast first. Knowing he was putting it off.

Andy looked forward to taking Jean to the movies tonight.

When he arrived to pick her up, Jean was dressed in a blue blouse with a matched sweater and pants set. He loved the look of her short-fluffed hair that was sun-streaked blond with a bit of gray in it.

"Wow you look fantastic!" He admired her.

"Thank you, kind sir." She came back meekly.

While the credits rolled on the screen and they waited for the theatre to clear out, Jean said,

"That was my kind of movie. Better than it sounded from the description."

Andy asked. "What part of the movie did you like best".

"The part where Julia was determined to get all her books read and win the competition. Even though it looked impossible with all the obstacles she had to overcome. She saw everything as a hindrance until she figured out that life had to be lived every day and there was time to read and do all the other chores by a set schedule. And the end when we found out her mother wanted her to win the competition so badly because she herself hadn't ever been able to do it. Then to find out she hadn't lived to see Julia win it was heartbreaking," Jean said.

The cool air felt good as they walked to the car. Jean said, "I made blueberry tarts this morning and I can make Columbian coffee or Earl Grey tea to go with them. How does that sound?"

He grinned, "No man in his right mind would turn down that offer."

"Columbian coffee or Earl Grey tea?" She asked.

"You choose the one you like best." He answered.

"Alright, I love my teas but Columbian coffee with the tarts," she said.

When they got to Jeans house, she served the treats. They ate and drank for a while with no words spoken. It was pleasant. Then Andy said, "I could get used to this peaceful time. These tarts and coffee are a wonderful combination. You are an excellent cook."

"Glad to please you," she said.

Andy looked sad and said, "It's hard to believe Dorothy is still living by a thread. She takes a turn for the worst then gets better. Dr. Greene mentioned that some people hold on like that and he has no way of knowing what the outcome will be. He didn't hold out any hope for her, but a miracle could happen."

Jean said, "I hate to lose her but since she has been under the heavy sedation for so long, she might be better off not coming out of it. She would hate to be in a vegetative state. Kept alive for years on machines. How do they know people can't feel pain when they are in that condition? We always want to give the patient time for a miracle or to come out of the injuries naturally. But no one knows what is best for them. How do you make those decisions? And yet, a plan must be made. So, a choice is made and the patient lives or dies by the conclusions made by someone else."

Andy reached out and took her hand in his and held it. Sparks flew, his pulse raced through his veins, and he was excited. He thought, *did Jean feel this too?*

"Better get going home. I've enjoyed this very much we'll have to do it again." He told her, rising from his chair.

She walked him to the door. And said, "Good night, Andy, this has been an exciting evening. Thank you."

Jean hesitated and Andy almost kissed her. *Was she waiting for him to kiss her*? Maybe. Andy was surprised at how quickly he had begun to care deeply for Jean and didn't want to hurt her. His confusion was connected to Dana Morrow and his inability to change that outcome. He had to be truthful with Jean and tell her what happened. Instead, he said, "Are you doing anything tomorrow?"

"Yes, I have plans with one of my widowed friends for shopping and dinner with her."

"Can I sit with you in church Sunday and take you to dinner afterward?" he said as he backed off the porch.

"Yes Andy. Tonight, was a treat. See you Sunday," she said.

"Good night, Jean." He got in his car and went home.

She made a point of saying her friend was a widow woman. *Did she do that to let him know she wasn't going out with anyone else*? He was in a happy frame of mind as he hoped that was why she did it.

Saturday Andy picked up his phone and started to call Jean then remembered she was spending the day with a friend.

Sunday, they met at church and then went to Sheila's for lunch. They knew many of the people waiting to be seated. So, the time was spent with several pleasant conversations. Andy felt it was another perfect day in Jean's company.

CHAPTER 14

Monday Andy answered the phone and said, "Hi Bob, what's going on? Anything new?"

Bob said, "Hi Andy, we found the van. It's burned out, in a field about two-hundred miles away. Our crew is on the way there now. Maybe they can find some information to lead us to the fugitives, who stole it. It was reported stolen a week ago when the owner got back from an Alaskan cruise and found it wasn't in the airport parking lot where he left it."

Andy said, "I sure hope the vehicle can tell us something."

Bob asked, "Do you want to meet me at Donavan's for lunch at twelve o'clock? Maybe we'll have more information by then.

"Sure, I'll be there. Bye." Andy eagerly told Bob and hung up.

Four hours to wait. He hoped the team could lift some prints or identify something to help find those child murderers!

He needed to do busy work to keep his mind off the wait time. He went to the cleaners with a load of clothes and got out the ones that were ready for him. Then made a stop at the florist and sent Jean a beautiful bouquet of varied colors of roses, carnations and three white football mums. He wrote her a note to be sent with them. He hoped she would love them.

Next was the weekly grocery store shopping. When he got home, he cleaned up the house. Then picked up his book and finished the fantasy world adventure, in time to go meet Bob.

He parked at Donavan's and went inside, sat in a booth and ordered his coffee. It arrived as Bob walked in the door.

"Hi, Bob is there any news?" Andy asked.

"Yes, the van didn't burn as thoroughly as the criminals had expected. Our team went over it and found some prints. We are running them now. Some blood was able to be lifted and it is being matched with Dana Morrow. That is all. It could prove to be a lot of evidence or nothing. The tests needed will take time. So, hang in and be patient." Bob said.

"Good advice but hard to do. It is that way with all our cases. Anything I can do to help?" Andy asked.

Bob said, "No, you're not officially on this case. We will get them." He continued, "I heard Dorothy took another turn for the worst. Her husband will have a public defender who is young, Anderson

Nelson, the third."

The waitress brought Bob's coffee and took their orders for hamburger and fries. Bob watched her walk away, then said, "I saw you and Jean going into the movie. You were so engrossed in talking to her that you didn't even see me. How are things going with her?"

Andy grinned, "She's great. I like being around her. But she is too good for the likes of me. I would not have thought that a while back. But I will have a hard time even getting her to look at me when she hears how I mishandled that case. I should just stop seeing Jean now before she finds out about it. She will never want to talk to me again." Andy lamented.

Bob answered him, "You are very repentant about what occurred. We might not have been able to do more even if the Amber Alert had gone out. You will have to forgive yourself in order to continue your job. Yes, your error in this event was bad. But we all make mistakes in judgement. You mourn the error calls and move forward. How many times have you given others that very same bit of advice?"

Evelyn came by with the coffee pot again and asked if they had enough or wanted dessert to top off the lunch. Both took more coffee but declined the cake and pastries. She picked up the empty plates and moved off.

Bob picked up his conversation as soon as she left them. "The way Jean looked at you I think she is already smitten. You might as well keep seeing her. She will either understand or not. You are both involved at this point, and you wouldn't be hurt more later than you would be now."

"You're right, I'm drawn to her and want to spend every minute I can with her, but I know she will be greatly disappointed in me when she learns the truth about how I let down Dana Morrow," Andy said.

Bob said, "I personally think she will understand. She knows the pressures we are all under.

And that we aren't perfect."

"I hope so," Andy said.

Bob tossed a sugar packet at him and said, "You must be in love. You've hardly eaten anything."

Bob was getting into his car and said, "I'll let you know when the reports are back. Bye for now."

Andy went home to wait. The time it takes for lab reports is always difficult. Usually there are several cases going so it is just part of your daily routine. Not working on this case was a challenge for Andy with his focus on only one case. On two if you add Dorothy's case to it. He would call Pastor Bill and see how she was doing.

When the phone was answered he said, "Hi, Bill. Anything new on Dorothy?"

Bill said, "Same as yesterday. No changes during the night. I can't see how she can hold on much longer. After all this time. Dr. Greene thinks her quality of life wouldn't be particularly good if she did come out of the coma. I'm in the miracle business and there is still hope. I have seen it happen. Many people are praying for her."

Bill continued, "I heard you and Jean are dating.

I'm glad for both of you."

Andy laughed and said, "Does everyone in the world know? It was only one movie so far."

"That's a good start." Bill said.

The rest of the week followed the same pattern. Meeting with Dr. Breen, two Al-Anon meetings and Andy talking nightly on the phone with Jean.

Saturday Bob met Andy at the Corner Coffee House. It was a cute sit-down place with wonderful designer coffee's, latte, cappuccino, and extra shots of espresso and flavors. They loved the home baked goodies that always tempted them.

Bob ordered, a double shot latte with a giant-sized apple fritter. And Andy ordered his favorite coffee and huge cinnamon bun. While they waited, they looked through the books for sale and trade. This was a great spot. You could read or start-up your laptop with their Wi-Fi or watch the big screen television. Or sit at different style tables or in the big comfortable chairs, with your friends over coffee and soup and salad or desserts. The owners were a friendly couple, and it had such a nice atmosphere, that people loved spending time here. Bob and Andy thought a coffee house should be exactly like this for the customers.

They were both avid readers. Their office partnership had been enhanced by their love of reading. They shared many common interests. They told people, "Reading makes us smart. How do you think we catch the criminals?" Then they grinned like smart alecks and laughed. Friends as partners work out well. And it had been good for them.

Tanya brought their orders and took their cards

and books to the register and brought back the bagged books and their cards and receipts to sign, then left them.

"Good news." Bob said after taking a big bite of his fritter and some coffee. "One of the prints found in the van were from Dana Morrow. Some of the blood also matched her." He took more coffee and fritter then continued, "Four of the prints belong to a juvenile offender. He has been off our radar for the last four years. Leon Younger, the one with the blue streaked hair. His records are sealed. We have sent out information to other states, hoping to get something back regarding his location for the last few years."

Bob handed Andy several photos.

Andy frowned and said, "Leon here fits Mr. Perkins description. The old man knew what he was talking about." He looked disheartened. "If only I had believed him! This makes my actions even worse. I should have had him looking at our criminal photo books. He might not have found anything, but I should have tried it." The police file photos weren't very good. When Andy handed them back to Bob they were burned into his memory.

"Bob, we need to find out if he had any friends or accomplices when he was arrested as a kid. Did you find any?" Andy asked.

"When we checked his old neighborhood, we found a few people who knew him or about him. One of the guys he ran with as a teenager is dead. Two others are being sought for crimes now. None of them fit the description of the other partner in this crime." Bob stated clearing his throat. "We are going to bring Mr. Perkins in to go over the books to see if he can find the second one, I don't know if he will be able to do it. He got out of the treatment center last week. We are looking for him. The half-way house where he was released hasn't seen him for two days. He may be drinking again. I'll let you know when we locate him."

They left the cozy coffee house. Said their, "Good-bye's." And went on their way.

Andy hoped the old man could remember. Maybe he can identify Leon Younger and his assistant. He had given good descriptions. Why didn't that fact get through to Andy's hard heart? If they get these killers, maybe then he can move forward. But if the case remains open, how will he handle that? *How can God forgive him*? He understood in his head that God can forgive, but his own feelings of not being able to forgive himself get in the way of his real belief in God's forgiveness.

CHAPTER 15

Bill called that same Saturday afternoon, "Andy, Dorothy died a few minutes ago. I am at the hospital with her son David. He's taking it real hard. Can you tell Jean?"

"Sure, Bill I'll talk to you later." Andy told him.

He made the call to Jean. "Can I come over for coffee, I'll bring cheese croissants from the Corner Coffee House."

"Good I'll start the coffee," she said.

When they were seated in her comfortable light-yellow kitchen, with the croissants in front of them, Andy said, "Bill asked me to tell you, Dorothy died a little while ago. He was with her son. They will let us know what arrangements are made for the funeral."

He watched her closely as he told her and noticed he was holding both of her hands. He didn't remember reaching for her. But this was good, he hoped it was a comfort to her as she cried silently. Jean wiped her tears on her cloth napkin. Then gave him a half smile.

"Thanks for holding my hands and being here to tell me. I did expect this to be the outcome. It is a shock when the final word comes down. Even when you think you're prepared. Why do you think it happens that way?" She knew there was no answer to that question.

They sat quietly drinking their coffee and eating the croissants.

Finally, Andy told her. I called Bob before coming over. He will let the prosecutor know. The charge against Charles Hill will be changed from attempted murder to murder. If his lawyer wants a plea bargain there will be evidence of pre-meditated, so he won't get it."

"He planned to kill her? I thought he had been drunk and was mad at her and it just happened. Premeditated makes it much worse." Jean shuddered as she said it.

Andy didn't know when he got up, but he was holding her now with her standing in the circle of his arms. He wanted to kiss her, but knew she wasn't ready for romance or anything else that went with it. She needed him to hold her only for comfort. She needs a friend not a lover. He continued to hold her and gently patted her shoulder, until she stepped back and pulled away. Jean went to the coffee pot and brought it over and poured full cups for them. They sat down and talked about everything and nothing, getting to know more about each other.

Bill came by Jean's house on his way home from the hospital. He told them about the funeral being set for next Saturday a week from today at10 A.M.

Jean made a light dinner for them of chicken salad sandwiches on homemade sourdough bread, chips, and raisin pie.

Bill continued talking. "I felt sorry for David Bentley, he felt he should have insisted his mother come live with him, when his father died." Bill looked tired; he ate a bite then went on. "I told him to place the blame where it belonged, on Charles Hill."

Bill finished his sandwich and took a few bites of the pie. "I hope he gets the maximum prison time allowed by the law, even the death penalty. I want the most extreme punishment possible."

They all agreed.

Jean said, "Dorothy was a lovely person, kind, generous and pretty. I will miss her terribly."

Bill said, "She was always dependable when we needed something done at church, she would do it. I imagine her funeral will be well attended by lots of friends. I forgot to tell you the visitation will be Friday at Fraker Funeral Home at 6:00 to 8:00 P.M.

Her son is flying home tonight. He'll be happy to get home again as his wife is ill. He will come back for the funeral and again for Charles Hill's trial. David is glad Dorothy had so many good friends. I need to go back to the church for some papers I need and then I can go home. Bye now."

They got up and walked him to the door. After Bill left Andy gave Jean a big hug and asked her,

"Would you like to go out to dinner tomorrow after church?"

She nodded, yes.

"Do you like Italian or Chinese food?" he asked.

"Both. Where do you want to go?" she asked.

"Donato's has great lasagna. I like the Golden Dragon for cashew chicken and their egg foo young is a favorite too. Which do you choose?" he asked.

"Golden Dragon, it has a beautiful interior. The pagoda roof outside is neat too. I enjoy the Koi fish under the bridge at the entrance. Since we're going to lunch after church, maybe you should pick me up here about 8:45 A.M.?"

Andy beamed, "Great, see you then." He gave her a quick hug and left. He whistled on the way home. Then he had to wait for tomorrow to see her again. He slept well.

Sunday morning when Jean opened the door, Andy stared a moment before he could speak. "You look great! I love all the different blues you usually wear but this red and black dress is stunning," he said. He took in the higher heeled shoes and matching black purse. She had changed her hair style a bit and had a dragon pin in it.

He said, "Jean you are a really beautiful woman."

"Thank you, kind sir. I think you are handsome." She blushed as she said it. "Would you like to come back here for pie and coffee after dinner. I have a lemon meringue pie."

"Ok," was his quick reply. That started their laughter.

After dinner they came back to Jean's house.

When they were seated at her table with pie and coffee in front of them, she said, "How can we have such an enjoyable day, out on a date, with good food, and lots of laughter when our friend has just died? Could it be a protective mechanism our mind creates to keep us sane?" She questioned as she looked deep into his brown eyes. An electric shock connected them for a moment. She broke off the look.

Andy frowned and thought about Dana Morrow. "Jean, I enjoy your company and would like to take our relationship farther and watch it grow into much more. But you don't know my bad side. You might not like me at all if you knew more about me. Maybe you would turn away in disgust, and never speak to me again." He stated.

"I can't think of anything that would change my mind about you," she said sincerely.

When he hugged her that evening, Andy hoped she was right about that.

Andy didn't get to see or talk to Jean on Monday.

CHAPTER 16

His meeting with Dr. Breen went ok. Andy was anxious to meet Jean at the Tuesday meeting. The Al-Anon Tuesday night meeting was spent mostly talking about the loss of their friend Dorothy Hill. Most of them knew her from church, some only knew she had attended a couple of their meetings. The fact that she was harmed right after she arrived home from one of them was very upsetting. It made their reason for being here more urgent to each of them. Get out if any abuse is happening. Resources for leaving were discussed again, along with the importance of keeping in touch with your sponsors. And the importance of making friends in the group to extend your options of help within the social structure of people going through what you have experienced.

Jean told them, "Dorothy's son David Bentley

had put her house for sale with a local realtor, Jenny Starling. They are asking two-point three million for the house. And that is below market value. They know they might need to lower it, since a crime was committed there."

Almost everyone had something to say and then they broke up for dessert and coffee. Andy told Jean, "If I keep eating the delicious food you create, I won't be able to fit into my clothes. Did your husband get fat after he married you?" They laughed.

"No, I don't think he gained any weight." She replied. "For you I can learn some fat-free recipes if you want me to."

"Never, no, no! I can exercise more and still enjoy the foods that taste so good," he said.

Andy liked that they laughed so much when they were together.

He thought, *Is this making plans for the future? I'd better be more careful in the way I say and do things. Jean still doesn't know about little Dana's death and my part in it.*

Friday evening came and Andy picked Jean up to take her to the visitation for Dorothy. She was wearing a traditional black dress and was sad and a little pale. He thought she was beautiful even though she was in mourning for her friend Dorothy Hill.

The funeral home furnishings gave a calming effect that was soothing to the soul. A great chandelier was placed exactly right and a gold plush round seat like you would see in a fancy hotel in an old movie invited you to sit there. The blue drapes and big vases with unusual arrangements with the gold framed mirror above the fireplace added to the ambience. These surroundings gave you a distraction when you're thinking got too heavy. Your eyes caught the gorgeous item or picture and helped create a peaceful atmosphere.

Andy leaned over and said into Jean's ear. "I know a larger number of people than I would have expected. I don't know all of the names but the faces of many of them are familiar."

"Yes, most of the church family are here and the Al-Anon members and others. David looks lost; however, he is greeting everyone. His wife has MS and couldn't travel with him. Sometimes she's fine but she's been having a bad time with it lately. This has been a painful year as she has needed more and more treatments. They have changed her medications without finding the one that works best for her. She can't drive any longer. Her mother is staying with her while David is here. They were thinking of having her move into their house with them. And now he thinks he should have moved his mother in with them when his father died. He feels guilty that she was left here to be killed by Charles Hill. David will be heading home as soon as the funeral is over tomorrow."

They attended the visitation Friday and Dorothy's funeral Saturday. The casket had been closed and speculation had gone the rounds about her condition. "She must still be bruised and looked really bad, or they would have opened it" had been one of the many comments. Most of the same people were in church Sunday. Andy liked this group. He and Jean spent a nice day together.

CHAPTER 17

Monday Bob called. "Nothing new to tell you on the case. Mr. Perkins has not been located, neither has Leon Younger.

"Sorry to hear that," Andy said. Listened a minute then said, "Okay, talk to you later."

He asked himself, *what was he waiting for? He had moved that letter, picked it up, put it down, more times than he wanted to count. Read it! Just read it!*

He reached out his hand and picked up the letter and took it to the kitchen table. Laid it down while getting a cup of coffee. He drank a big gulp of the hot liquid and used the letter opener. Gently removed the letter. Still not sure he wanted to read the pages from his father.

Read it, he had to. Now is the time, do it. The letter is dated four years ago. It has been here that long? He didn't think it was so far back.

"Dear Andrew,
My Son,
I have joined Alcoholics Anonymous. This is exceedingly difficult sitting down to write, now. I have been putting it off. Writing to you is one of the steps I must work my way through to complete my healing. I can't see how you can forgive me. I treated you and your mother badly. My life has been drinking, violent rages, blackouts, and not remembering what happened. I did apologize for hurting your mother, repeatedly. She cried and cried. I am terribly sorry. I didn't understand that the words I was using with her, and you were as bad as if I had been beating you both. Now I do see that words can hurt and make a person shrivel up inside.

I hope it is not too late for you to find forgiveness for me. Somehow, maybe this will be possible for you. Please try. When I was sober, I loved both you and your mother. Drinking took away everything. Selfishness was all there was room for in my life. I failed you at every turn. I failed myself.

I have a job at Hillmont Greens Golf Course. I handle the golf shop. Do you play golf? I hope you can forgive me. I would like to talk to you, but I will wait to hear from you. If I don't hear anything from you, I would not blame you. I have always been so proud of you. Knowing that you became a well-respected police officer and that you did not take after me, has meant a lot to me. They say it is in the

genes and so I am glad you did not get that from me.
Bye now.,
Love,
Your Dad.
P.S. My address is: 777 Bluebell Circle. Mitchell, MO 63777.

Andy wanted to throw something but didn't want to have to pick it up or replace it. He was angry and sad, yet also glad the letter had been finally read. *Now what? Should he check out the address and contact his dad? Was he ready to forgive him? Could he really forgive his dad?*

Andy needed forgiveness too. His crime is worse. A child died. Andy wanted to be free of his sins but didn't want to forgive his father. *How can he get what was needed if he didn't give his father what he needs?*

Check and see if this is a correct address. Check and see if he is still working at the golf course. Then Andy can decide what to do next.

"Hillmont Country Club, how may I direct your call?" the nice female voice asked.

"Is Sean Palmer, working in the golf shop?" he inquired.

"Yes, I am connecting you."

The phone was ringing. Hang up. It is being answered. Andy was almost panicky.

"Hillmont Greens Golf Shop," his father said.

"Dad, this is Andy," he said nervously.

"Son, I had almost given up hope of hearing from you. Can you forgive me?"

"I'm not sure about forgiveness yet. Dad, could we have dinner sometime?"

"Sure, just say where and when." excitement showed in his voice.

"Do you know Knight's Restaurant on Madison Street?"

"Sure, I have been there. Love the roast beef dinner."

"How about7:00 P.M. this Friday?" Andy asked.

"Good for me. I will be looking forward to seeing you. Thanks. I look a lot older, and I am sure you do too."

"Yes, Dad, bye."

"Bye Son."

They both hung up the phone.

What will happen next? Andy wondered.

Tuesday, he told Doctor Breen, about the letter. And the call to his dad. Only to be asked how he felt about it?

"I'm not sure what to think. Guess we have to meet and see how things go from there," he said with uncertainty.

He had looked forward all day to seeing Jean at the meeting. He waited for her in the church parking lot. "Thought you would never get here," he said.

"I am not that late, am I?" she questioned.

"No, I wanted to see you is all."

Andy shared the information with the group. "My father sent me a letter four years ago. He was in Alcoholics Anonymous and following the steps. I opened it yesterday and called the golf shop where he said he was working. He was there and I decided to meet him for dinner this Friday. I do not know how I feel about this turn of events. I'm so angry for all the wasted years of his drinking, and shouting, and belittling. But, I know I have to forgive him. I don't want to do it. Wait and see, seems to be the thing to do." The group congratulated him on making two big steps. Reading his father's letter and contacting him.

Jean invited him to dinner Wednesday evening.

"Of course, only because you are such an appealing cook. I can hardly wait for tomorrow." He teased. Feeling good he returned home.

Andy didn't remember having many friends. He never considered the give and take worth his time. He gave his time to the Al-Anon group and received from these people, talking, laughing, fun, advice, and good companionship. This is a gift he'd always taken for granted. Hopefully never again. It is nice to call people, friend.

Wednesday evening, he stood on Jean's porch with a box of chocolates and a gardenia plant, Andy rang the doorbell.

"Hi," she said as she opened the door and waited for him to enter. She held her breath, as he passed her.

He handed her the plant and set the candy on the arm of the nearest chair.

"I love gardenias! How could you know? Candy, too? What wonderful surprises." She hugged him fiercely.

They talked easily and enjoyed the evening and each other's companionship.

Andy said, "That was a fantastic dinner. Pork chops cooked in cranberry sauce isn't anything I have tried, it sure was good. You said it cooked all day in the slow cooker?"

"Yes, that way they fall off the bone. I like to serve them with mashed potatoes and spoon a little of the sauce on them as gravy, add a small salad and you have a nice meal."

"Are you ready for dessert?" she asked. I have apple pie with peppermint-stick ice cream, or some zucchini bread left from last night."

"Apple pie." he grinned like a happy kid. He sighed when she sat it in front of him.

At the door Andy kissed her on the cheek and thanked her for the wonderful dinner and told her he would see her at the meeting tomorrow. After Thursday's meeting he called her, and they talked an hour on the phone. He finally got some sleep.

All day Friday Andy wondered how the evening would go with his father. He decided he would tell him how he'd made him feel all these years.

Sean Palmer was sitting in the waiting area when Andy arrived at Knight's Restaurant. They were seated right away. The waiter took their order and brought their drinks, iced tea.

Andy's father opened the conversation with, "I have been sober almost five years now. A friend helped me get into the AA Program I attend regularly. I have sponsored several people who have been successful with their problem. My greatest hope is that you will be able to forgive me and that I can make amends to you. I was thrilled to get your phone call and even more grateful that you wanted to meet tonight. It has been too long not seeing you. Since I had written the letter so long ago, I almost gave up hope that you would contact me. I thought you might have thrown it away."

Andy said, "I planned all day to tell you how much you hurt me and Mom and blow off steam. But I am glad to hear that you are successful with your sobriety. I am in a mandatory Al-Anon program, I think it is helping me. Like with Mom there is no way to correct what I did. I have been one of the best detectives in our department. Recently an old drunk came in and reported a child had been snatched in front of him. I didn't think he really saw what he was telling me. I chalked it up to him being a drunk and wanting a warm place to sleep for a few days. So, I arranged for him to go to the Alcoholic Unit. I did check and found no missing child had been reported. I didn't put out an amber alert. In a few days, a vehicle was reported missing like the one the old man told me about. The owner arrived at the airport and found his van had been stolen. The old man had given me a partial license plate that matched. The girl was found in a dumpster.

My boss put me on a month's leave and sent me to a shrink and Al-Anon. One of the things we were told to do as an assignment was to forgive and make up with people who had harmed you or you had harmed.

I remembered your letter I had thrown into a drawer. It took me a few days before I was willing to get it out and open it. I'm glad I did and hope we can build up to a relationship. Right now, I'm still very angry at you. I hold it against you that Mom didn't have chemo so she could die and get away from us. I know that my being able to be forgiven for Little Dana Morrows death, I in turn have to forgive you. But I'm not ready to do it."

Andy had run out of steam. The waitress brought their orders. They talked a long time and enjoyed the meal together and made plans to meet again and see if they could mend the years of strife.

"Thanks for coming tonight," Andy said.

He got into his car and wanted to scream. The meeting with his father wasn't so bad but he wasn't ready to forgive and forget.

Saturday, he did his yard and called Jean. "Hey there, I'm restless would you want to roam around some backroads with me?"

"Sure, I can be ready in a half hour. Jeans and sweater ok or were you stopping somewhere? she asked..

"Figured we'd just drive and maybe eat at a fast-food place on the way back."

When he pulled into the driveway Jean came out to the car and got into it. He said, "You take my breath away. You are so pretty."

She responded with a big smile and thanked him. "I haven't been on an outing to see the land and wildflowers for a long time. Once when we were going for a day trip, I picked a beautiful rose and held it sniffing it. When we got to our destination, I put it in the cup holder, and we locked the car. It was a hot day and when we got back in the car the rose had shrunk but it was perfectly preserved and hadn't lost any of its color. I placed it in a small vase and kept it for years. It was a great reminder of that lovely day."

Jean asked, "How did the evening with your father go. I hope it was good."

He frowned. "It went well. But I'm still not wanting to get over all that happened and forgive and forget. I know I have to get to that point for myself. But I don't want to do it. I told him we would get together again. It may take me a while before I'm ready to see him again. And it probably won't be over food. I had a hard time swallowing it."

"That's a good start. It doesn't have to be instant. Ask God to help you handle it. He will you know," Jean said.

They were having a great time roaming old country roads and finding some of them now had been made into housing tracts. They discovered a nice family restaurant and had lunch. Andy enjoyed the easy conversation. He opened up about what a neat woman his mother had been. She loved to dance and caught on to the new steps of the dances that were popular when he was growing up. At the end of the day Andy stood on Jean's porch and asked to kiss her. She nodded yes. It was brief and wonderful. He wanted it to last forever but knew he had to tell her about Dana, before he could let this go on any farther. But he didn't tell her. He went home and told her he'd take her to lunch after church tomorrow and would pick her up to go with him for Sunday School.

Sunday Andy picked up Jean for church and lunch. He was sharing more with her and growing fonder of her each time they got together.

CHAPTER 18

Monday Bob called. "Good news. The juvenile records have been opened and Leon Younger has an Aunt Maria Antonio who is now living in a large, elegant home for several retired women. They have a housekeeper, cook and a maid to take care of them. I have an appointment for 2 P.M. Can you meet me at the Corner Coffee House so we can ride over in my car?"

"Yes. Thanks for letting me be in on your interview with her. What about the people he ran around with in his juvenile years, are there any other leads?"

"Yes, I'll bring the photos. See you at 12:45 at the coffee house. Bye now."

Andy was so excited that Bob was involving him in the case. They always worked well together. He hoped the aunt could tell them something that could lead to Leon Younger's capture. Andy was early and had finished a coffee already when Bob came in the door and headed straight for his table. Tanya followed him and asked for his order.

Bob opened his folder and brought out three photos of former friends of Leon. "Todd Manning, Vern Talbot, and Edward Belton had all been arrested with Leon Younger on a robbery charge. We are trying to find current addresses on them."

They finished their coffee and pastries and paid the bill and got into Bob's car for the drive to Maria Antonio's home. It was a huge old mansion, with flowers and trees surrounding it. There was a large, elegant sign in front that said, The Willow Tree. The doorbell was answered by a maid.

Bob told her they had an appointment with Maria Antonio at 2:00 P.M. She moved aside and invited them to enter. She led them to a parlor and asked them to be seated and she would announce their arrival to Mrs. Antonio.

A tall elegantly dressed and coifed woman entered. She had been beautiful and still had the essence of it. She introduced herself and they did the same and she sat down. "How can I help you? Mr. Simon mentioned wanting to speak to me about my nephew Leon Younger. What has he done that you are interested in him?"

Bob said, "We think he was involved in the theft of a van and possible homicide. When did you see Leon last?"

"Those are more serious charges than the things he got into in his juvenile days. It was about a month ago that he came here. He came asking for money, since I must be rich to live in such a place as this home. Leon expected me to give him $1,000.00 a month. He had only found out about me when his mother died. His good for nothing father told him to get out and get his due from his mother's rich sister. He told Leon who I was and where I was living. He kept track of me over the years in case I became handy for a loan," she said.

The maid brought tea for them and poured it and passed out cookies to go with it. They enjoyed the tea and cookies. Maria continued. "I had read about my sister's death in the newspaper but didn't go to the funeral. She and I had a big quarrel when she married Earl Younger. I have kept up with their doings too. Leon was in trouble almost from the time he was born."

Bob asked. "Did you say Leon's father's name was Earl Younger?Do you have his address?"

Maria reached in her burgundy suit jacket pocket and brought out a lovely piece of stationary with a beautiful handwriting on it, with the information they needed and handed it to him. "I thought you might need that," she said.

Bob thanked her and asked, "Did you give him any money?"

"No, I told him to go and apply for a job. And if he could prove to me, he had gotten a real job, I would give him food money until his first paycheck came in. He was incredibly angry and bunched up his fist. I told him the maid would call the police if he didn't leave right now. Susie, our maid, had come to stand in the doorway holding onto her phone, because she heard our loud voices. He left but shouted at me on his way out, that I hadn't heard the last of him. He really frightened me."

Bob asked. "Do you know what kind of vehicle he came in and if he was with anyone else?"

"No, but Susie might have seen it." Maria rang a little bell, and the maid came into the room. Maria introduced the detectives.

Bob asked. "About a month ago Mrs. Antonio had a visit from a nephew, and you stood by her with your phone ready to help out. Do you remember if he had anyone with him or see what kind of vehicle he drove?"

"Yes sir, I wrote it down on my notebook. I will go get it and be right back." Susie said.

She wasn't gone long and when she came back, she handed Bob the notebook with the page open to the car type, color, and license plate number. She had written, Leon, Mrs. Antonio's nephew. She also had noted he called out "Danny lets go." As he got in the car. He made a fist, threatening he was going to hit Mrs. Antonio. I will watch out for him in case he comes back. If he does, I will call for help right away.

Bob smiled and thanked her for all the information. He asked her to continue looking out for Leon and told her it was important to report it right away and gave her, his and Andy's cards. He also gave the cards to Mrs. Antonio.

Susie followed them out the door and shut it. Bob thanked her and asked if he could check with her on Mrs. Antonio's well-being. She gave him her private phone number and indicated she would be happy to help in any way possible. Bob asked her last name.

"Moyer" she said.

Bob drove them back to the Corner Coffee House. On the way Andy had called in and had an officer checking on the car and license number. They went in and had more coffee and another big apple fritter. Andy's phone rang. "Hi Andy, I got the info on the car and license. The 2002 Toyota Corolla, blue is registered to Daniel Howard at 1032 E. Battlefield Road, Apt. 12, Springfield, MO 60004. Hope this helps."

They got back in Bob's car, and drove to Daniel Howard's apartment building. First, they went to the manager's office and introduced themselves to Mr. Richards. He told them, "Daniel Howard had been kicked out of the building about three weeks ago for non-payment. We had to evict him. I have no idea where he went. His friend was really mean and threatened several of the other tenants."

"Do you think one of the tenants would know where they went?" Andy asked.

"I don't think so. No one wanted to know them. You're welcome to ask them." Mr. Richards said.

"Can we see his apartment?" Andy asked.

"I'm sorry, we went in as soon as he was gone and made repairs and rented it within a week. The new tenant is nice, you can ask him if you think there might be anything left to find." the manager said.

"Thanks for your help. We will be around awhile if you think of anything." Bob told him.

They spent the next three hours questioning the

tenants who were at home. No one had anything good to say about the young men. Several mentioned being afraid of the boys. The new tenant let them into the apartment, but they found nothing, and the young couple hadn't found anything during the time they lived there.

The manager stepped out of his office when they got there and handed them a kitchen towel with a knife and gun wrapped in it. He told them it had been left with a pile of clothes and a video game that came out of Mr. Howard's apartment. His wife had reminded him about it after the detectives started talking to the other tenants. He was sorry the clothes and game had been donated, but they had kept these items.

They thanked the manager and left. Bob said, "It's been a long day. I'm ready to go home. Would you like to go with me tomorrow to check out Leon's father?"

"Of course, I will. What time do you want me to meet you?" Andy said.

"Two will be good." Bob pulled into the Corner Coffee House parking lot next to Andy's car. "I'll pick you up here and we can have coffee before we go. Thanks for being there today. I'll check the gun and knife into forensics evidence and punch out for the day. Bye now."

Tuesday Andy had made arrangements with Bob to meet at the coffee house after his appointment with Dr. Breen.

The shrink appointment went well. Andy told him about the mostly positive meeting with his father and that they would stay in touch with each other. But that he was still angry and didn't want to forgive him.

At 2:00 P.M. Andy pulled into the coffee house parking lot right behind Bob. They went inside together and sat in a booth. Tanya took their orders.

Bob said, "The address Mrs. Antonio gave me looks good for Earl Younger. I also have the addresses for the three boys Leon was arrested with as a juvenile. We have a busy afternoon ahead of us. You said you have a meeting tonight, didn't you?"

"Yes, on the meeting. Glad so much is coming together. I have to finish this before we can go though." Andy answered.

Bob smiled. "Of course, I wasn't leaving my apple fritter either."

Earl Younger stepped out on his porch as they drove up. He waited for them to get out and speak.

Bob asked. "Are you Earl Younger?"

He said he was and invited them inside. They followed him and he told them to sit down. The house was lived in but clean, which surprised them. Bob introduced both of them.

Mr. Younger said, "You must be looking for my lazy no-good son, Leon. What's he done now?"

Bob answered him. "We are investigating the theft of a van and murder. When did you last see Leon and do you know where he can be located?"

"Wow, I knew he was rotten, but murder is something else. Are you sure it was him?"

"Right now, we just want to find him for questioning then we'll go from there. He visited his Aunt Maria Antonio. He frightened her and told her you had told him to go mooch off his rich Aunt.

What can you tell us?" Bob asked.

Earl said, "Maria was in my class, three years ahead of her sister Marta. When I got interested in Marta, Maria knew all the bad things I had done. I sold a little bit of drugs and was in many fights on campus, stole things. I got caught and put in juvie for a while." he paused. He asks if they would like anything to drink and when they said no, he went into the kitchen and brought back a bottle of water and drank some of it. Then continued.

"Maria told Marta all about me and she still fell for me. Maria wouldn't come to the wedding and the two sisters had a big argument and never contacted one another again. I kept track of Maria hoping they might make up the loss. It hurt my wife very much. I worked hard for my family but never quite had enough money to make it a good living. Leon was too much like me and was always in trouble. We thought and prayed he would outgrow it."

Earl went on, "After his mother died, he just laid around the house and brought his friends over. I told him to go mooch off someone else and get out of my house if he wouldn't work and help pay for food and clothes. I didn't know he had found the book I had written in about Maria being his mother's rich b.... sister, it had her address. I guess that is how he found her. I'm sorry he frightened her."

He drank more water and said, "I haven't heard anything from him since he left. That was about two months ago."

Bob and Andy thanked him and left their cards in case Leon contacted him.

As they drove away Bob said, "He surprised me, even though he has a clean record since his juvie days, I wasn't expecting a pleasant man. My mind pictured him as a brute."

Andy said, "I hadn't expected a clean house and a hardworking man. Where are we headed next?"

To interview Todd Manning, one of the boys arrested with Leon and sent to juvenile hall. No other complaints on him. He now has a real estate office on Sunshine so we will go there. Hope he is in today and not out showing a property. His office was located in a nice building with several other business offices. His receptionist greeted them and asked how she could help. Bob asked her if Todd Manning was in and could give them a little of his time. She smiled and said one moment. She punched a keypad and announced to Todd he had customers waiting for him. They heard him tell her he would be right out front. He appeared almost immediately. He invited them back to his office.

Bob introduced himself and Andy.

Todd asked what they needed from him. When they told him, it was about Leon and the theft arrest he turned red and stammered. "I thought those records had been sealed."

Bob assured him they were still sealed and only opened by a court order in order to help them find Leon Younger.

"I haven't seen or heard from him in years. Juvie was bad enough for me. I have never done anything else that could get me arrested again. I am a good salesman, and have built a great business and have a wonderful wife and kids. I would never put any of that in jeopardy." Todd told the detectives.

Andy asked. "What about the two others you were arrested with, have you seen them?"

"I ran into Vern Talbot in the grocery store about five years ago. He told me he had gotten a job in a car dealership in Canada. His uncle was a friend of the owner. He thought it was a big opportunity for him and his wife and two kids. They were buying snacks on the way out of town, for the long drive." Todd said.

He continued, "I see Edward Belton and his family at church. He is our pastor at Saint Paul's Methodist."

Todd tapped his pen on the tablet on the desk. "You haven't told me what Leon has done. He was mean as a kid, I guess he has gotten worse. It must be really serious if two detectives are here."

"We want to question him about the theft of a van and a possible murder." Bob told him. They left after giving him their cards.

As they drove away Bob said, "That was pretty much what I expected from Todd. From the information I got on the three of them his statements went along with what information I had."

Edward Belton and his family lived in a lovely, modest house next to Saint Paul's Church where he was the pastor. He answered the door at the house and invited them inside. He introduced his wife Pauline; she smiled and ask if they would like coffee.

Bob introduced himself and Andy and told her thanks but no on the coffee. They were all seated.

Bob came to the point of the visit. "We are hoping you can help us find Leon Younger. We need to question him on the theft of a vehicle and a murder. Do you know anything about him in recent years?"

"I haven't seen him since we got out of juvie. He told us we were wimps when we told him we wouldn't go along with any more of his schemes. He could continue as a criminal if he wanted, but we were going to do all we could never to be in a situation like that again.

About a year ago I ran into Sylvio Barra. He told me he had seen Leon and another man Harlan Avery, in a bar. They bragged about getting out of jail in Wyoming. Sylvio and his friends told them good luck and left the bar. That is the last I have heard about Leon. I hope that can help you."

The detectives thanked the Belton's and left their cards.

Andy said, "Isn't Sylvio Barra that big lawyer?"

"Yes, the same. He has a good reputation for being fair. I heard he decides if his client is guilty. If he is, Sylvio won't take the case unless there are unique circumstances." Bob said.

Bob was pulling into the Corner Coffee House lot when his phone rang. He parked and answered it. The call was the reply to one he had placed yesterday to the Canadian police in Vancouver. Information was given and records sent to the office on Vern Talbot. He was licensed to sell vehicles and was specializing in motor homes. No problems since he had been there during the last six years.

Next, Bob called the office. "Bill, any news yet on Jonathan Perkins?"

He hung up and told Andy, "The old man hasn't been located. They will keep looking for him."

Andy said, "Bob, thanks for letting me go with you today. I think I will hang around the shelters and see if I can pick up any information on Jonathan Perkins. Someone might know something that the officials running them might not know about. Let me know if you hear anything."

"Be careful. We have been asking about Leon and it may get back to him. If they saw Jonathan when he saw them, he might be in danger. I'll keep you updated. Bye now. Hope you have good luck in finding that old man." Bob said.

CHAPTER 19

Andy drove to the homeless shelter and parked about a block away, and one street over. He surveyed the area and then got out of his car. He walked around and talked to a few men sitting on the ground. After about an hour he was tired and thought he would call it a day.

A man wearing a jaunty gray hat with a small fan shaped blue feather in the band, followed him to his car. "I heard you are asking about Jonathan Perkins, trying to locate him. You're a cop, aren't you?" He asked.

"Yes, I am, Andrew Palmer." He showed the man his badge. "What can you tell me about Mr. Perkins?"

"Are you looking for him regarding that little girl who died?"

Andy said, "Yes, do you have any idea where I

might find him?"

"He told everyone that he saw her snatched. No one believed him until we heard about her death. After all, he was just a crazy old drunk, a street bum. He cried when he heard she was dead. Then he stopped talking at all. I'm Carman De Lorna, I work at the hospital where he was sent to dry out. He quickly sobered up and was sent to the rehab facility. He left there one night, and no one has seen him since. I'm afraid that if he saw the people who took her so clearly, they might be after him."

Mr. De Lorna took out a cigarette and offered one to Andy who refused. He lit his own and took in a long inhale of smoke then let it out before he spoke again. "I've been talking to the men on the streets, and no one admits to seeing him. Several of them know me so I think if they knew anything they would have told me. Now we have many of the street people afraid for his life. The only good thing from that is they will be on the lookout for those two punks. I hope that boy doesn't change his hair color. I hope you find Jonathan and those killers."

"Mr. De Lorna thanks for talking to these homeless people. Now that they know their friend might be in danger someone might come forward. We have spoken to the shelter people, and no one had any information."

Andy said, "Good-bye."

He was tired and looked at the time and headed to the meeting. Andy got to the Tuesday night Al-Anon meeting after it had started so he didn't get to talk to Jean until it was over. They talked a bit then he walked her to her car, and he went home. He tossed and turned again all night.

Early Wednesday morning Bob called. They had a meeting at McDonald's on Kearney Street. When they entered, they looked around. Bob spotted her first. Mrs. Delia Ferguson wearing a sunflower on her straw hat. That is how she told the dispatcher she would be known by the detectives.

Bob introduced them to Mrs. Ferguson and asked how they could help her.

She said, "I hope I can help you. I heard you needed to find Mr. Jonathan Perkins. I have known him many years. He was very distraught over that poor dead child. I saw a couple of guys that fit his description of the punks he saw take her. They were cruising the neighborhoods looking everyone over good." She coughed and paused awhile.

Bob smiled at her and asked, "Can I get you something to drink and eat?"

She said, "That would be nice. A large coffee and a sausage egg muffin with some hash-browns please."

Bob placed the order and got them both coffee to share with her. He brought it to the table and told her to go ahead and eat it while it was still warm.

She nodded gratefully, thanked him, and started to eat. When she was finished, Bob got them all coffee refills. Mrs. Ferguson started talking again. "Those punks were in an ugly brown van."

Bob wrote it down.

Mrs. Ferguson said, "Since I saw those boys, looking over the homeless people, I think Jonathan needs you to find him. I think the kids were looking for him. Mr. De Lorna mentioned that since he had given good ID information that the killers might have gotten that good of a look at him and might come looking for him. That scared all of us." She paused and drank the last of her coffee.

Bob refilled their coffees and asked if she wanted anything else to eat. She said, "Four of those sausage muffins to go would be nice." Bob got them for her and bought her a $20.00 Mc Donald's gift card.

Tears came to her eyes when Bob handed her the food and gift card. When she was able to speak, she said, "I didn't ask you to meet me here to have you buy me food and pay for more food. But, thank you so much. I wanted to tell you what I know about Jonathan. He told me a few years ago that he has a daughter here in town. She and her husband both have good jobs, and he left their house because he didn't want to be a burden to them. I think he was scared enough to have called her to come and get him. He once gave me her name and phone number in case he died, so she would know what happened to him. Mrs. Ferguson handed Bob a paper with the information written on it.

Bob and Andy thanked her and gave her their cards and told her to call them if she needed anything. They left and drove away and were anxious to find out about Jonathan's daughter. Andy opened his computer and found out a lot of information. Betty Jo Perkins Barker had a phone listed and her home address on Southern Hills Blvd. She was employed as an office manager for Donalee & Donalee Law Firm. Her husband Brent Barker was employed as Assistant Manager of

Portman's Bank.

Bob pulled into a shopping center parking lot, and they discussed their plan of action. Andy told him all he had found out about the background on Jonathan Perkins's daughter and her husband. And said, "If we go to the house when the daughter isn't home Jonathan, if he is there won't open the door. He might bolt, and we won't find him. I think we should talk to the daughter first. Her husband might not be that helpful. Do you think we should go to the law firm and talk to Betty Jo Barker?"

Bob thought that would be best. Donalee & Donalee offices were on Primrose in one of those fancy buildings. Inside was elegantly furnished. Bob asked the receptionist if they could speak to Betty Jo Barker, and he introduced himself and Andy. Mrs. Barker told her to send them back to her office.

Betty Jo was well groomed and dressed in a conservative light blue suit that matched her eyes. She had a calm about her that immediately made you comfortable in her presence. After the introductions were made, she said, "Please be seated. How can I help you?"

Andy answered her. "We believe your father, Jonathan Perkins, might be in danger and we are looking for him. We also need his help to solve one of our cases."

Betty Jo said, "So he really did see that child snatched and the police didn't believe him and sent him to an alcohol treatment center?"

Andy felt his face grow hot and said, "Yes, ma'am that is what happened. I was the one he talked to that night. I did check the missing reports and she wasn't on it. I checked the partial plate he gave me and didn't find anything. He admitted he was homeless and had been drinking a lot that day. I thought I was doing him a good deed getting him some help. I have regretted it ever since that child was found."

Mrs. Barker said, "You did help him. He has stopped drinking. But he is afraid those boys will find him and kill him. He is back home at my house again. He left because he thought he was imposing on us. I hope we have convinced him that we would rather have him with us. He has a nice apartment in the lower floor that walks out."

She continued, "How did you find me?"

Andy said, "A woman he knows, Mrs. Delia Ferguson was afraid for him. The homeless people knew that if he saw the boys so clearly, they might have seen him and come to harm him. She had seen a couple of guys that were looking over all the homeless people and thought it might be the ones he told us about. A few years ago, your father had given her your name and phone number in case he died on the streets, so you would know what happened. She thought he might have been scared enough to have called you to come and pick him up. Is that what happened?"

"Yes, he took a cab to Battlefield Mall and met me outside at the food court entrance. Can you wait until I get off work?" She looked at her wall clock and said, "I will be home about 6:00 P.M. Or do we need to go to Dad now?"

Bob said, "It would be best if we can go now and

take you with us. We didn't want to show up at the house while you were working because we didn't think he would open the door. We were afraid he would run and we wouldn't find him. We want to show him our photo books so he can help us find those criminals. I hope he is still willing to help us."

"I can take off. I am sure he will want to help, since that is what he wanted all along. Do you mind if I drive my own car and you can follow me?" Betty Jo said.

The investigators followed Jonathan's daughter in her burgundy Cadillac to her lovely home. They got out of the cars, and she led them to the downstairs apartment and rang the bell. The door was opened by Jonathan Perkins.

He said, "Hi Betty Jo, I see you brought company."

She introduced the detectives. He invited them to sit down and offered fresh coffee. No one accepted.

Jonathan asked, "Are you ready to accept my help now detective Palmer? By not believing me that night you made me realize how far down I had come in society. I was once a particularly good lawyer in Boston, before alcohol took over my life and I lost everything. I moved out here to be near my daughter during a sober time. When I started drinking again, I felt it was putting a strain on Betty Jo and Brent's marriage. That is when I became a street person, homeless. I plan to stay sober this time. So, thank you for sending me to the treatment center. Why are you here today? If I can help, I will be glad to do so."

Bob said, "We are sorry to have let you down.

Your information has been extremely helpful. The vehicle wasn't reported stolen for several days because the owner was on vacation. When he got to the airport parking lot, he found it was gone. The little girl hadn't been reported as missing yet because her mother worked late and didn't know she wasn't home waiting for her. Detective Palmer checked all these things while you were in our office."

Andy said, "Mr. Perkins, you have good friends in the homeless community who were worried that those boys might kill you. They thought if you got that good of a look at the criminals, they might have had that good of a look at you. It is a good thing you gave your daughter Betty Jo's information to Mrs. Ferguson. She saw a couple of guys looking too close at the homeless population and was afraid for you, too. She met with us and told us about your daughter Betty Jo."

Jonathan said, "Sometimes the area is safe and sometimes dangerous. Having friends helps. Delia was once a surgical nurse, well respected in her career. Her husband died with lots of debts, and she lost everything and ended up on the street. When I told her about Betty Jo and Brent, she had just lost a friend and told me I should make sure Betty Jo was notified if anything happened to me. I gave her the information and forgot about it."

Bob said, "We would like you to look at our photo ID books and see if you can find those murderers in them."

"I'd be glad to do it. When do you want me to be there?"

Bob said, "If it is ok with you, we want to put you into protective custody since there is evidence that they are searching the homeless people for you."

"Ok, that will be fine."

Bob made the arrangements on the phone. They took Jonathan to the station to try and identify the culprits. He paged through several photo books and picked out Leon Younger. He didn't find the second man. He was tired by the time they took him to the safe house. They left him there with a couple of guards.

Andy said, "It's amazing to think, Mr. Perkins used to be a lawyer. He sure looked different today all clean and well dressed."

Bob said, "It is amazing to find out about the street people. Delia Ferguson was a surgical nurse. It must be hard for them to remember who they once were and knowing how far down they have come."

They went for coffee. Bob said, "I saw Brad talking to you but didn't hear what he said. He looked happy to see you there."

"Yes, he was glad you were keeping me in the loop and that I was able to help. He was afraid you might not want anything to do with me, so you allowing me to assist was welcomed. Thanks for not shutting me out. Where do we go from here with the investigation?"

"I may have picked up a lead. While you talked to Brad, Lou Breeze gave me some information. It seems there have been a rash of convenience store and liquor store robberies in the last two weeks. The guys come in with masks on and tell the clerk to, "Be smart and hand over the cash, one more dead body doesn't matter to us." They enter from the side of the store and run out the same way. No visible getaway vehicle. After one of the robberies the boys ran into and knocked down an older man. He waved his cane at the nearest one and knocked his hat off and saw a blue streak of hair. He thought it might be the ones the homeless community was looking out for because of their friend Jonathan. When he got to the store the police were arriving and he told them about the boys running into him. He hadn't seen them get into a car. They had kept running after knocking him down. Lou gave me the contact information for Mr. Williams. I thought we might talk to him Friday. I know Thursday is your meeting night." Bob said.

"Yes, and I was taking Jean on a picnic to the park on Thursday, so Friday is good for me to meet you and talk to Mr. Williams. Maybe he will have thought of something else. So, shall we meet at the Corner Coffee Shop?" Andy asked.

"No, Mr. Donald Williams lives near the water tower on Pine Street. I called and told him we would be there Friday at 10:00 A.M. How about meeting him first then have lunch at Sheila's Place?"

"Good idea, on Fridays, Sheila's usually has that fish basket I like. We could meet at Sheila's for breakfast and leave one of the cars there when we go to Mr. Williams' home then go back for lunch."

"Andy that is a good plan. I have to go by the station first and will meet you at Sheila's about 8:30

A.M." Bob said.

Thursday, Andy and Jean had an ideal afternoon at the park.

That night the Al-Anon meeting had a special guest. Pastor Bill introduced the speaker.

"I have known this special person for many years and her story always inspires me. I want you to give a big hand to Amy Trenton."

Amy stood before them looking beautiful, which was odd because she wasn't beautiful. However, the inner presence of her being glowed.

She said, "I think of myself as Amy Trenton Spy."

"I always loved the sound of that. It came to me on my first trip to the hospital with a broken arm. I had been warned within an inch of my life that I had better stick to the story that I had been clumsy and fallen off the porch and landed on it. That didn't account for all the bruises on my body, but I made it sound plausible. After all, I was supposed to be a klutz.

I pretended that as a spy I was being interrogated by the enemy forces and the candy sucker I was given by one of the nurses when we left, was a medal of honor. I had passed my spy test. After many years of pretending to be Amy Trenton Spy Extraordinaire my tormentor died in a knife fight in a bar. My mother had died when I was about ten years old and now my father was dead.

I had been slipping into church for years hoping my spy ability made me invisible. Brother Bill kept trying to draw me out, but I ran away from him. He came with the police when my father died. I was sixteen almost seventeen and I insisted I could take care of myself. Brother Bill became my guardian and got me into his first Al-Anon meetings.

Amy Trenton Spy worked for me as a child. Al-Anon let me live a good life as an adult. May your experiences here make your lives better each day. Forgive and let go of hurts and memories for your own sake. Concentrate your time and energies to making good new memories to take into your future."

"When I became a lawyer and advocate for abused people, I was surprised at the number of men who are abused by wives and children. Usually, I find that their mother told them, "Don't ever hit a woman." I'm convinced the mother meant don't become a man that abuses women. But he has taken it to mean never under any circumstance hit a woman. So, he becomes the abused person."

"If you know of anyone male or female being abused or even suspect it, talk to them. Tell them to get out. There are places where they can get help. Verbal abuse can lead to thoughts of suicide. Speak up if you are concerned about someone. On the table by the coffee, I have placed several brochures with locations for abuse help. Please take several. Read them and make yourself aware of them. Memorize the information. You never know when you can tell someone where to go for help. They may not want to take a brochure that could start another beating if found by the wrong person."

Andy and Jean talked about the meeting and Jean told him she had prior commitments for Friday and Saturday. They planned to have lunch together after church on Sunday at Jimm's Steakhouse. He would pick her up for church then after the service they would drive to the restaurant.

CHAPTER 20

Friday morning, Mr. Williams opened the door and said, "Right on time. I like that. Come in and be seated. Can I get you coffee or something?"

"No thanks." Bob answered. He and Andy found seats and looked around. It was a comfortable home with a cheery atmosphere. They were ready to question him.

"Please tell us all you know about the robbery suspects, Mr. Williams," Andy said.

"I was walking to the convenience store and these two thugs ran right into me knocking me down and laughing about it. I hit one with my cane and his cap came off and his blue streaked hair showed. They kept running. It is hard to get up off the ground, so it took me awhile to do it. Then I continued to the store and found out it had been robbed apparently by those two who ran me down. I told the policeman about their interaction with me. After arriving home, I remembered a van I had seen in the neighborhood a few days before. It kept going up and down my street. I had written down part of the license because it looked suspicious." He went to a small table that held mail and a vase and picked up a tablet and handed it to Andy. He continued "It was a brown van with a sliding side door. I don't know the make of the vehicle. In the olden days I could tell them all apart, each had distinction. Now they all look alike. You can't even tell a Ford from a Chevy. Old man Ford is probably turning over in his grave."

Bob asked, "How did you know the homeless people were looking out for the blue haired guy?"

"A couple of the men sleep on my porch sometimes. When they do and are still around when I get up, I give them coffee and bacon and toast. And we talk. Some of them have amazing stories. I don't know how much to believe but they can weave some tall tales. One of them told me about the blue streaked hair guy and that they had been looking too closely at all the homeless people. Since my wife died it gets lonely. I have good neighbors, but they work most of the time. I hope this will help you find those punks."

When they arrived back at Sheila's for lunch several other officers were already there. Bob and Andy sat in the car while Bob gave the information on the brown van to the office and then went into the restaurant. Their fellow officers invited them to sit with them and added a couple of chairs to the round table.

Karl Kelly said, "Andrew Palmer the great detective of our time, you sure blew it with the little school girl case."

"Karl you are right. I did a bad job of it. I'm hoping we can catch those murderers. We are working it and just now got another lead to follow up," Andy said.

Billy Jones said, "I've thought a lot about it. Any of us could have missed on that one. Think about it we all thought the same as Andy. We were all tired and felt he was just and old drunk telling tales. None of us spoke up that night and said, "'Wait, he might have seen what he says he saw.'" I have also been thinking about the vehicles the guys used. The first was stolen from the long-term parking at the airport. Maybe we should periodically check it. They might be in the mood to pick up another one. And they might leave the old one in the lot."

Bob said, "Good idea Billy. We will check that out. We got a partial license on a brown van with sliding side door a few minutes ago. The numbers are being checked now." Everyone talked as they ate lunch.

When they were leaving the restaurant, Bob said, "I'll go back to the office and check out the stolen car lists again and see if anything is going on at the airport. I'll let you know whatever I find out. Maybe you'll think of something we need to follow up on. Have a good weekend. Bye for now."

Andy drove home. He called and made the reservation for 1:00 P.M. Sunday at Jimm's Steakhouse. Reservations aren't required but they are busy on Sunday after church, so he wanted to be prepared and not have to wait in a long line. He caught up on his mail and did some yard work.

Saturday Andy went to the store where a free sample day was in progress with many people giving out product samples, mostly food. He tried pizza, ice cream, soda pop, pretzels, quiche, and other things and he left with a slight stomachache. He got everything on his list and added several of the sampled items too. When his chores around the house were done, he read for several hours.

Friday and Saturday Jean was busy all day, but Andy got to talk to her on the phone each evening. These calls were getting longer and longer. Saturday, he had another restless night and was anxious to see Jean again this morning.

Andy got up and dressed for church, made breakfast, and read his bible until time to pick up Jean. The church service was a good one about forgiveness, and they chatted on the long drive to the restaurant.

Jean said, "That sermon hit me hard. The hardest person to forgive is ourselves. And even though we know God has forgiven us when we ask him, we sometimes go back and pick up that memory and struggle with it wondering why it went that way. I'm still working on that problem."

Andrew knew this was the time he should tell her about the big mistake he made resulting in little Dana's death. He hadn't been able to forgive himself even though he had asked God's forgiveness. *Would she be able to forgive him, or would that revelation end their growing relationship?* He chided himself for being a coward.

But still didn't tell her."

He told the restaurant hostess, "I made a reservation, my name is Andrew Palmer."

She seated them right away and took their drink orders, as people waiting looked at them.

Jean looked around and said, "This is my first time here, I love how it is broken down into several small intimate rooms with comfortable seats. I have heard the food is wonderful. Will you order for me? It is so hard to decide what to choose."

"How does this sound to you, start with shrimp cocktail, then lobster, asparagus, and baked potato and split two desserts, layers of chocolate cake with chocolate mousse, and layers of white cake with blueberries, cranberries and rich creamy lemon mascarpone?

"Oh, I like all of those. That is a lot of food. Can we eat it all?"

"I know I can, I'm that hungry. If you can't we can take it home in a to-go box."

The waitress came back with new cups of coffee and took their order. Andy added four brownies to go.

Jean said, "I was almost finished with the first coffee and really like that she brought new cups when she came to take the orders."

They talked and ate and enjoyed each other's company. They used the restrooms before getting back in the car for the trip home.

Jean said, "I want to take the ladies who help me with the flowers to Jimm's for coffee or tea and dessert soon. I know they will love it too."

Andy stopped mid-sentence as they watched the

big semi crash through the barrier lines on the west bound lane into their eastbound lane and hit a van that had no way of escaping. The impact pushed it into the car beside it and a couple of other vehicles smashed into them.

Andy pulled over onto the shoulder and told Jean to use his police radio to report the accident and get the needed personnel rolling. He put several flares in the road.

She picked up the mike and keyed it. He was already running to the accident scene. "How may I help you officer?" From working with her Jean knew the voice. "Chloe this is Jean. Detective Andrew Palmer is on the scene of an accident and asked me to call it in. Roll everything. A semi and several vehicles are involved. We just passed mile marker ninety-four in the eastbound lane. The accident is ahead of us.

"Ok, Jean, they are on the way. Stay safe." Chloe said.

"Thanks Chloe, I'm sitting on the sidelines and will pray for all those people." Jean put the mike back in its holder and started to pray. She saw a lot of action when the police, ambulances, fire department, sheriff's officers, and tow trucks arrived. It took about three hours to clear the scene. Jean was glad they had used the restroom at the restaurant before starting home.

Andy finally came back and got into the car. He asked if she was ok and when she nodded yes, he thanked her for the helpers arriving so quickly. Then told her, "The coroner thinks the truck driver had a heart attack and was dead when he hit the guardrails. He was the only fatality. Several were taken to the hospital and several others slightly injured. Five vehicles were towed."

He took her home and gave her two of the brownies, walked her to the door and declined the offer to come in for coffee. He smiled, said goodbye, and headed to his house.

When Andy got home, he tried to read but that didn't work. He was tired, but it was too early to go to bed. The guilt was eating away at him.

Andy knew he was acting like a coward by his inability to tell Jean about what happened to Dana because his father had been a drunk when he was growing up. He hadn't heard the truth of Mr. Perkins insistence that Andy must believe him and find her.

He had just proved his ability to take the needed actions at the accident scene and do the job that needed to be done. And he had followed through with Dorothy Hill's case. Bob was glad to have him helping on Dana's case now. But how could he ever make up for his failure with Dana. He wouldn't be able to get much sleep again with all the turmoil filling his mind. He had to try to sleep tonight. He was in hopes they could make some progress on finding Leon and his pal tomorrow.

CHAPTER 21

Monday Bob called, "I need you to meet me. I'm at the Cash and Go on Hampton Blvd. The clerk/owner shot one of the robbers. I don't think it was the blue haired Leon."

"I'll be there as soon as I can." Andy hung up.

Bob came outside to talk to Andy when he arrived. "Hi, thanks for getting here so soon. We traced the blood about a block over on the next street where they must have had their vehicle parked. The blood stopped at the curb. The boy must have been hurt pretty bad judging by the blood loss. He will need a doctor or hospital. We alerted the hospitals and paramedics, and a bulletin went out to the area doctors."

The store owner David Menkle, said they came in with black knit masks and guns and told him to, "Be calm and hand over the cash, one more dead body doesn't mean anything to us." Mr. Menkle pulled up his gun and the robber holding the gun shouted, "You're dead." Mr. Menkle shot him and the other one drug his friend out of there. Since they were leaving, he didn't shoot the second one.

When they left the crime scene the detectives went to the station. Shortly after they were seated Bob's phone rang.

The caller said, "911 This is Susie at Marie Antonio's home. I have an emergency, send the paramedics." The phone line went dead.

Bob called the dispatcher and said, "This is detective Bob Simons, connect me with John Markham at the fire station and stay on the line."

"Hi John, we need paramedics at The Willow Tree, 1592 Mariposa Lane. I want you to be there. I think our murder suspects robbed the Cash and Go and are there. One of the young men was shot by the storeowner a short time ago. This may be a hostage situation."

"Ok, Bob. We're on our way. See you there."

Bob then told the dispatcher to send the patrol cars code two, no lights, or sirens. He and Andy went to his car. On their way Bob said, "I've been keeping in touch with Susie at the Willow Tree. It must be Leon since she called me instead of 911. I wonder how she got that past him?"

Susie met them at the curb. "Leon's gone. He dumped his friend Dan and shot out the electric box and smashed my phone." She was walking them around the back as she talked. The paramedics arrived and followed them to the back.

The cook had been sitting beside the bleeding

boy talking soothingly to him. She moved so the men could work on him.

Bob asked. "How did you get my number dialed and pass it off as a 911 call?"

She said, "When he drove up and stopped. I dialed your number. Leon struggled getting him out of the van and when he saw the phone in my hand, he asked what I thought I was doing. I told him his friend was bleeding, so I was calling 911. That's when you answered. He let me make the call then grabbed my phone and smashed it on the driveway. He went to the fuse box and shot it several times. The electric went out. Leon ran to his car and left. I got the Missouri license number, ARZ332. Liz, our cook came out and I told her what happened, and she went in and told the ladies we were safe, and the police and paramedics were on the way. Then she came back to sit with the boy, so I could go wait for you in front and direct you back here."

Bob said, "You did good. I'm glad you're safe."

Susie said, "Bob he said the hospital had cops swarming it so he brought him here because he couldn't think of anywhere else."

Andy came back to them. "Bob are you ready to go? The paramedics are moving him now to Mercy Hospital. He's asking for a priest. John doesn't think he has much chance to come out of this. He has lost so much blood. He gave me his information. So, we can make some connections."

Andy nodded at Susie and said, "You did us a great service calling Bob direct. We knew Leon Younger must be here. We're glad you weren't hurt. We'll have a couple of the cops stay here in case

Leon might come back here since he couldn't think of anywhere else to go." After he said that he went back to the car.

Bob said, "Could I take you out to dinner sometime soon? I've been wanting to ask for a while now."

She said, "I'd like that. I'm off on Wednesdays and Sunday."

"Do you prefer Italian like Zio's, or Steaks at Longhorn's?"

"I've never been to either. Let's try Zio's and then if we want, we can try another time for the steakhouse. What do you think?"

"I like your idea. Wednesday I'll pick you up at 7 P.M. and we'll go to Zio's. It's a date, see you then. Bye now." Bob said. He whistled a happy tune on the way to the car.

Andy watched his partner walking to the car. When he got in, Andy said, "Where are you two going on your date?"

Bob turned and looked at him. "What makes you think we are going on a date?"

"You looked happy coming to the car. I was here when you saw Susie the first time we came to speak to Maria. That time you made sure she had all your phone numbers and you have mentioned keeping in touch with her. I'm your partner, you know you can't keep secrets from me."

Bob said, "She's so cute and I feel protective toward her. We're going to Zio's, Wednesday evening. Now you know it all. Let's go to the hospital. I hope that boy survives so we can talk to him."

They sat in the surgery waiting room because the criminal, Daniel Howard, was there to get the bullet removed.

Bob said, "You and I will have a long wait here it seems. How is it going with Jean?"

Andy said, "Fine, I enjoy spending time with her. I still haven't told her about Dana. I'm afraid she will hate me when she hears about it. And I know I need to tell her soon before we find that thug. I hope we can catch Leon Younger soon."

While they sat in the surgery waiting room, a priest entered and came over to introduce himself. "Are you Palmer and Simons?" He asked.

"Yes, we are." Bob said.

"I'm Father Benedict of Saint Anne's Church. Your criminal spoke to me before going into surgery. He instructed me to tell the police his confession if he doesn't make it out of surgery. If he comes through it, then I must remain silent. So, we will wait. Mary Ann just made fresh coffee; I'll be glad to bring you some when I get mine. How do you take it?"

Andy said, "Black for both of us. Thank you, we can use it right now."

The coffee was good and strong and just hit the spot. The three men talked while they waited. After about three hours Dr. Kaplan Greene came in and spoke to them. "Glad to see all of you again, I wish it were under better circumstances. Daniel Howard made it through the surgery but he's not going to live long. He's in the Surgery ICU. You can go now and speak to him. He doesn't want his accomplice to get away with their crimes if he has to die." He smiled and walked away.

The three men went to the room where the patient waited. He was still a bit groggy.

Father Benedict asked, if they needed him to wait while they spoke to the young man.

Bob said, "He might talk easier with you here since he already gave you his confession. If we need you to leave, we will ask you to do so."

A nurse spoke to them when they entered and told her who they wanted to see. She said, "Dr. Greene said you would be in to see him and not to give you limits, since he doesn't have much time. Come this way." She led them to a bed.

The boy was hooked up to numerous machines that made different noises. His eyes were open, and he looked scared.

The priest said, "Danny do you remember talking to me before the surgery? And that I heard your confession and that I gave you the last rites before you went into surgery?"

"Yes. The doctor said, there was too much damage done to my insides for me to live and I'm afraid of dying. I told you I did bad things. If I die before I can tell this, you have to tell them. I don't want Leon Younger to get away with murder when I have to die. He is pure evil. I didn't touch that little girl. I drove the van that's all."

All the machines went haywire and beeped and flat lined. Doctors and nurses rushed in and pushed them out of the small space. Daniel Howard was stabilized about five minutes and then he was gone.

Father Benedict said, "I'm tired. Can you come to my home, and we can have dinner? My housekeeper has made a big pot of spaghetti today. And I can tell you what Daniel told me before the surgery."

Andy said, "Sure that would be good."

Father Benedict lived in a nice house next to Saint Anne's. It was cozy inside and smelled of good food. The housekeeper Margaret greeted them and invited them to wash up and come to the dining room where she served supper. She placed salads and bread sticks before them. Andy asked. "How did you know to make so much food?"

She laughed and said, "Father always brings company when I make spaghetti. I'm not sure if he thinks it is the best in the world or if he hates it and doesn't want leftovers."

Father Benedict said, "It's the best, of course."

After the four of them ate, the men went to the priest's study and he told them what he knew about, Daniel Howard.

A day or two after the body of Dana Morrow was discovered. I found a young man in the confession booth crying. He kept repeating, "I never touched that little girl. Leon Younger did it, and then he killed her. I'm so sorry."

A few days later he was back and said, "Leon's going to kill me. He says I have to kill someone so I can't tell on him. Or he will have to kill me himself so I can't rat him out. He wants us to rob convenience stores to get money. He gave me a gun and wants me to use it on one of the clerks. I know how mean he is and I'm sure he will kill me."

I told Daniel he should go to the police, and he said, "I guess it would be better to have Leon kill me than go to prison where they would know I drove the van when the child was killed. I've heard prisoners do really bad things to people who kill children."

Today, John Markham, the paramedic, called from the ambulance and told me Daniel had asked for me and wanted me to meet them at Mercy Hospital Emergency Room. I arrived shortly after they did. I was able to talk to him and give him Last Rites before they took him to surgery.

I taped his confession, so I'll play it for you. He put the hand-held recorder on the desk and started it. "This is Father Benedict from Saint Anne's Parish. Recording a confession for…Please state your full name young man."

"Daniel Edwin Howard, I talked to you at the church, so you know what I told you before. If I die, I want you to tell the police. If I live you can't say anything until I'm dead. Leon Younger got me taking drugs with him after his friend Harlan left for Canada. They had been in jail in Wyoming together.

Leon and I stole a van from the airport parking lot. I was driving a few days later and he said to pull over and I did. He grabbed that child and started yelling for me to "'Move It!'" She fought and screamed until he hit her and knocked her out. We drove a long time. I walked a long way from the van and was sitting outside on the ground in a deserted area when he raped and killed her. I cried for her, and me.

Leon came to find me and started hitting me and calling me names and threatened to kill me if I didn't do as he said. We drove back to the city, and he put her tiny body in the dumpster. I was sick for days.

One minute, Leon acted like we were best friends and the next he threatened to kill me. After he dragged me out of the store, he yelled at me that I was supposed to kill the old guy and called me all kind of names. When we got in the van he became my best friend trying to get me to a hospital. We went to both ER's and the cops were all over the place. He said he would go back and kill the guy that shot me and his family too. Father, you have to let the police know that man and his family needs protection right away. I think Leon will go there now.

Then he thought of his aunt's place and dumped me there. I think my getting shot made him crazier than he was already.

Father, I was holding the gun on the old guy and told him he was dead, and he lifted his gun over the counter and shot me. I couldn't believe he shot me. That wasn't supposed to happen. He shot me. Thanks Father for hearing my confession."

Father Benedict stopped the tape and said, "That is when I gave him the Last Rites and he was taken to surgery."

Andy said, "Since Daniel told you to tell the police about the store owner and his family needing protection, why did you have Margaret call it in anonymously?"

"It was included in a confession, and I thought it would be better to do it that way. Police were alerted and there would be no reprisals about it being in a confession. And you and Bob heard him tell me to notify the police if he died, I had no problem letting you hear his confession."

Andy said, "You handled it well Father Benedict. We had protection on another person who interacted with Leon, tThe store owner would have been covered, but we didn't think he would go after the man's family."

Bob drove them back to the station to pick up Andy's car. Bob left and Andy looked at his phone. It was still early enough he could call Jean. He knew he had to tell her about Dana. She answered and told him she would be glad to have him come over right away.

CHAPTER 22

Jean invited him in and led the way to the living area where they sat in the chairs by the fireplace. This was the room Andy liked the best of what he'd seen of her home.

Andy said, "Jean I have to tell you some things and want you to let me tell it all before you say anything. I hope what I tell you won't make you hate me. I had planned to ask you out on a date several times when I came back to your office for coffee. But it didn't happen. Then when I met up with you at the Al-Anon meetings everything seemed to work out. I have grown very fond of you. More than that actually. But, my secret is causing me much distress."

He continued. "I let my personal life interfere with my job. An old drunk came into the station telling what I thought was a pink elephant story. It was like I was snapped back to my father's drunken actions. I resented the old man and his taking up my time with this ploy to get attention. I did check the partial license against the stolen vehicle list and for children reported missing but found nothing. I set up a place for him to get treatment. And told my partner Bob not to worry about it. I was sure Jonathan Perkins was just an old drunk looking for a warm place to get off the streets awhile.

A couple days later Captain Bradley called, and I had to go to the morgue and see the body of the child that was abducted, and I had ignored the witness's story. Little Dana Morrow will never be forgotten by me. I'll always feel guilty for letting her down. If I had put out an Amber Alert, could she have been saved? I didn't do it, so we'll never know. The old drunk gave a perfect identifiable description of the two boys. I should have had him looking through the photo books to see if he could identify the boys who took her.

The captain told me to take a month off and attend Al-Anon meetings and see a shrink he arranged. I couldn't see how that was going to help me. It seems the shrink, Doctor Breen only knows one sentence, "'How do you feel about that?'"

Through Al-Anon I saw I had to forgive my father so I could be forgiven and be able to forgive myself. That was hard because I didn't want to forgive him. But now I was the one who needed forgiving.

These boys have been robbing convenience stores and today one of them was shot by the owner. He died in the hospital. He had given Father

Benedict from Saint Anne's permission to tell his confession after he died so Leon Younger, the killer, of Dana Morrow would go to jail. If he had to die, he wanted Leon not to get away from the police.

We have leads on Leon now that weren't there until this event. We are moving fast and want to capture him right away. I wanted to let you know what I had done and ask your forgiveness before we brought him in, and everyone knew about my part in the investigation. I would like for you and me to have a long-lasting relationship but I'm afraid this information might come between us." He slumped in the chair and didn't say anything else. He had watched her as he told his tale of woe but couldn't tell how she was taking it. She had sat looking at him with an unreadable expression on her face not showing her feelings.

Jean said, "I think we need a good strong cup of coffee and a piece of chocolate cake. Come with me and then I will tell you what I think about what you told me."

He followed her to the kitchen and sat at the table while she prepared the coffee and cake. It seemed the time dragged on, and his stress level was going higher each second.

Jean said, "Let's eat and talk later." When she finished the last bite of cake and refilled their coffee cups she said, "I work in the same building as you. Our grapevine is probably one of the most active in the state. I have known all about the night you didn't believe Jonathan Perkins drunken story. Every officer who was there that night knew it could have been them that made that same decision and that they had also believed as you did that, he wanted off the streets. I have wanted to reach out to you and tell you it would be ok. But that wouldn't have helped. I knew you had to come to the place where you could tell me about it and decide you could continue your job as a detective. I see you are fired up to catch Leon Younger. That is what Brad wanted to see in you. He is glad Bob still wants to be your partner and that you two are working together even though you are supposed to be off.

I want to see where our relationship goes from here now that you are back to your confident self. I'm sure Dana Morrow will always have an effect on you, but you will use it to be an even better detective.

I'm glad you will have a relationship with your father now that you have a way to channel your anger about his previous actions. Al-Anon will continue with your growth and you will be able to help many people by sponsoring them." She looked him in the eye and reached out and covered his hand with hers and smiled.

Andy said, "I was so afraid you would hate me. I've been so disgusted with myself for my actions. Thank you for having such a beautiful soul."

Andy said, "Bob and I took Jonathan Perkins in to look at the photo books of arrested criminals and he picked out Leon Younger. When we saw Daniel Howard the other man today he fit his description perfectly. That made my guilt worse. We found out Jonathan got sober and plans to stay that way. His daughter and son-in-law have respectable jobs and he now lives in the walk-out apartment downstairs in their lovely house. He was a renowned lawyer until his drinking got the best of him. The homeless woman who made it possible for us to locate him had been a surgical nurse. This time has brought some surprises and been a learning experience for me. I hope I'll never again judge anyone by their outward appearances."

Andy stood up and so did Jean. He moved closer and took her in his arms and kissed her long and passionately. He felt so many things during this kiss. When it ended, he continued to hold her in his arms. He bowed his head and said, "Dear Lord, thank you for putting this lovely wise woman in my life when I needed her the most. Bless our relationship. I pray that we will catch Leon Younger before he harms anyone else. Thank you for loving us. Amen."

He told Jean goodnight and that he would see her at the Al-Anon meeting tomorrow night and went home to get some rest.

CHAPTER 23

When Andy got up on Tuesday, he called Bob to see if anything had happened during the night with Leon Younger. Nothing to report. Mr. Minkle and his family had been safe and nothing suspicious had occurred.

The meeting with Dr. Breen went well. Andy told him about the advancement and that they had a new lead to catch Leon. And about his talk with Jean and her positive reaction.

Andy didn't get to the Al-Anon meeting that night. Bob called and he hurried to the Minkle home. One of the officers watching the house reported a suspicious car that had cruised the street a couple of times. It was a silver Chevrolet Corsica. That didn't fit because Leon usually drove a van. The officer insisted they needed to follow up on it. He had gotten a partial plate and when it was run through their process it came back as being owned by a Jessica Summers who lived in the next county over. Probably another vehicle stolen from the airport.

Several officers were outside and inside the Minkle's house. An officer assigned to follow Mr. Minkle from work spotted a silver car following him almost home then it turned off and lost the officer. Nothing else happened that night.

Wednesday morning at shift change Bob and Andy went home to get some rest so they could come back tonight for another watch over the Minkle Family. When they met at the office, they found out that the car the officer had recorded the license number for was supposed to be in the airport long term lot. One of the day officers had reached the owner Mrs. Summers and she was in Italy for business and wouldn't be back until next Monday night.

Officers were looking at the airport trying to find the van that Leon had been using. Maybe if he took Mrs. Summers car, he left the van there. After a thorough search it wasn't found.

"Detective Bob Simons," he said into the phone.

"Hi Bob. This is Gary Taylor. I just went off duty and stopped at Jenna's Bar and Grill to pick up some dinner to go and ran into an old friend, Damon Zahn. He told me, he works at the hospital and heard we were looking for Leon Younger who you thought was with Daniel Howard when he was shot.

Damon said, in junior high school Leon called himself, The Tiger. The kids turned it into Tony the

Tiger from the cereal fame. Many of the kids who called him that got beaten severely. Leon bought drugs from Nicky DeTello. He is still selling them, and I would bet Leon is one of his customers."

"Commercial Street is where we usually find Nicky. We've arrested him several times. My partner and I will check it out tomorrow. If you want us to do that."

"Yes, please do it. Thanks for your information. "Bob turned off the speaker phone.

About 6:00 P. M. they followed Mr. Minkle home from the convenience store. All they had to report the next morning was another unproductive night.

Bob had been quiet and not happy about having to postpone his date with Susie so he could work the stakeout.

Thursday before heading to the department to meet up with Bob, Andy called Jean and let her know he would miss another Al-Anon meeting tonight due to work. The loneliness he felt when he didn't see her was new to him.

He and Bob were sent to an address on a homicide call before it was time to go follow Mr. Minkle home. They had been there before. It was Earl Younger's home.

Officer Jim Scott met them at the door and said, "The neighbor Mr. Troy called us and thought he heard gun shots. He told the dispatcher he wouldn't go check on his friend because he had a violent son, and he thought the boy was crazy. He had heard some arguing before the shots but went to make his land line call from his kitchen to us. He didn't see anyone leave the house.

When we got here the front and back doors were both open. We entered and found Mr. Younger dead on the living room floor. No one else was in the house. The coroner and his people are in there now."

Andy asked, "Have you spoken to Mr. Troy?"

"Yes, he plays cards with Mr. Younger on Friday nights and is very distraught over his death. He said the boy, Leon had been bad ever since he knew him. Always in some kind of trouble or other but he didn't think about him killing his father."

Andy asks, "Why does he think Leon killed him?"

"He had seen him arrive and sneak into the house a few hours before his dad got off work. He and another boy had been doing that for about a month and always left before Earl got home. He didn't tell on him because one of the first times it happened, he saw him watching out the window and came over and threatened to kill him if he told his father. He assured him, he wasn't doing anything harmful and was just playing his video games while his father was working. I think today his father came home early and found him there."

Andy thanked Officer Scott.

They went into the house and made notes on the scene before them and spoke to the coroner and found out Mr. Earl Younger had been hit by four bullets from a short distance away from him.

Next door they spoke to Mr. Albert Troy. He was a retired Navy man. He didn't add much to what he had already told Officer Scott.

The other neighbors were interviewed, and all had good words about Earl Younger but nothing good about his son. His death shocked them all. One woman summed it up for all their feelings. "When something like this happens our feeling of safety living in our own home is shattered."

It was about 9:00 P.M. by the time Bob and Andy arrived at the Minkle home to relieve the officers who had covered for them when they were called to the other crime scene.

Andy noted it was 11:43 A.M. when he poured them both more coffee from his thermos. They sat quietly drinking it. In a few more minutes he would make another round of the area on foot and check on the other officers watching the house. Bob had done that about an hour and fifteen minutes ago.

Bob said, "I wish we could get this case wrapped up tonight. I made another date for Sunday with Susie. Are you going to church with Jean again?"

"That's the plan. I talked to her about my mess up with Jonathan Perkins and she was so nice about it. She had already heard about it through the work grapevine. I hadn't even thought about that happening. She seems to want to see where our relationship goes from here."

"Good, I'm happy for you."

"I better do my round of the area." Andy got out of the car and started down the block. Nothing seemed to be moving. All was quiet until he got about four houses from the Minkle's place. He saw a slight shadow on the house. Andy stood still as a statue. It felt like a long wait before the shadow moved forward toward a fence. The body climbed over the top and dropped into the yard and ran across it and climbed the next fence and dropped over. Andy was in front of the houses and moved along with the stealthy figure. He opened his phone and quietly let Bob know they were heading his way.

Bob sent a heads-up notice to the others.

When Leon arrived at the Minkle's back door he was surrounded by police. Andy took his gun away and arrested him. The boy broke down and started to cry. And then shouted. "That old man in there killed my only friend. He and his family have to die."

At the police station Leon claimed he didn't know his father was dead and didn't do it. Why would he kill his father he asked the detectives. Then he would tell them he needed to kill all the Minkle family because Mr. Minkle had killed his only friend.

Leon repeatedly asked them why Mr. Minkle wasn't being interrogated about killing Danny. It was like being on a carousel going around and around but not getting anywhere. After several hours they locked him in a cell and went home.

Friday when Andy got to his desk there was a newspaper on it. Bob asked, "Have you seen the newspaper? Mr. Minkle was interviewed."

"No, since all this started, I've avoided all media."

"Read it then." Bob said.

Andy took the time to do it after taking his coat off and hanging it he sat in his chair and read.

The reporter Tim Newman asked. "Mr. Minkle,

when you shot the robber a couple of days ago did you think his partner might come after you and your family?"

Mr. Minkle said, "The police told me afterward that he might try to kill us because the boy I shot had told them that his partner in crime would do it. I thought I was doing the right thing not shooting the second guy. I let him haul his friend away. I thought I had stopped a robbery. I didn't know they had come there to kill me. If I had killed the second one, then he wouldn't have had a chance to kill his own father.

I will shoot anyone involved if it ever happens again. If anyone out there has ever thought of robbing my store, don't do it." The article went on to tell about Mr. Minkle having been a sniper in the military and more about his family.

While Andy read the news article, Bob had taken a call from Officer Gary Taylor. He and his partner had Nicky De Tello at their desk if they wanted to come over and talk to him. For immunity he was willing to tell them what he knew about Leon Younger.

What he knew wasn't much. Just about Leon's drug buys and long-time habit. He would testify in court if they needed him.

A public defender had been assigned to Leon and he would be meeting him today. For now, their part of the case was over. Bob and Andy were looking forward to their dates on Sunday and hoped to be able to unwind tomorrow.

Saturday, Andy spent his day working in the garden and relaxing. Before bed he called Jean and they spoke a couple of hours. He told her. "I'll pick you up for church in the morning. Bye."

Sunday morning Pastor Bill greeted Susie and was introduced to Bob Simon. The pastor said, "Haven't I seen you at the hospital with Andy Palmer?"

Bob said, "Of course, that's where I've seen you. He's, my partner. We just finished a case we were working on. You were at the hospital with Jean and Andy waiting to find out about Dorothy Hill, weren't you?"

"Yes, I heard her case will be tried in the court in the next few weeks. It's a sad business. Andy and Jean Baughman are sitting about mid church at the center aisle if you want to sit with them." Pastor Bill said.

Bob looked at Susie and asked her if that would be ok. She smiled and said, "Sure, I know Jean Bauman and that would be fine."

Andy looked up and smiled when he saw Bob and Susie. He said, "You told me you were taking Susie to her church, but I didn't know it was this one."

Bob laughed, "I didn't know either. Small world, our girls know each other. Can we sit with you?"

Andy and Jean moved over and gave them the end space. Jean said, "You have to come home for lunch with us. Pastor and his wife will be there too."

Bob said, "We planned to go to Zio's for lunch."

Jean said, "I insist, Sunday in a restaurant is too crowded. You can go there anytime. I want to show off my cooking skills. It's my mother's meatloaf recipe that I claim is the world's best and cherry cheesecake for dessert."

Bob looked at Susie and asked if she would like to have dinner at Jean's house and go to Zio's another time. She smiled and nodded. He said, "Jean, that is totally unfair. How could we possibly turn down such a meal? But how do we get through the sermon thinking about the food that waits for us?"

They were still chuckling when the song leader introduced the man doing the announcements for the week.

Late that evening Andrew Palmer said, "Today your house was filled with joy and laughter and wonderful food. I feel we have been really blessed. I want more days like this."

He kissed Jean and she said, "I want that too."

THE END

ABOUT THE AUTHOR

Janet Kay Gallagher is a Christian Author. Both my parents were readers, and my earliest memories are filled with fun trips to the library. My parents read the BIBLE and the CHILDREN'S CLASSIC STORIES to my brother Bob and I before bed. In the days before television, the newspaper and radio were our news and entertainment. Sunday morning, we ran out and got the newspaper and jumped in bed with Dad and Mom, and Dad read the comics to us. Like some of our favorites, TERRY AND THE PIRATES, DICK TRACY, LIL'ABNER, and DAGWOOD AND BLONDIE. Later in the day he would read items from the newspaper about trees and planets and anything of interest.

Two librarians had a positive impact on my reading. Mrs. Warren made sure I was reading the books in my age group, she knew if I had checked them out to read. I was impressed by the personal care and guidance of Mrs. Warren.

I loved Mrs. Tierney's Seventh Grade Library

Training Class. Checking out books and working in the school library was fun. Mrs. Tierney gave personal attention to the books I read and discussed them with me.

I enjoyed reading to my two boys Stephen and Ken. When Stephen was in fourth grade I was told he had Dyslexia. That explained my own reading problems. And why the librarians helping

keep my reading up to my grade levels meant so much to me. When I was in school it didn't have a name. Mom couldn't understand why I couldn't tell the difference in, The and the, since they were the same word.

I still read daily or listen to books read by my Kindle Fire. I'm also a big fan of Audiobooks.

Now I'm writing short stories and poems and my own books. I hope my readers will enjoy them and remember the stories.

Watch for new releases from Janet and
find her on Facebook
https://www.facebook.com/janetkay.gallagher

Also by Janet

Three talismans, The ring of Valor, the Emerald of Truth and the Amulet of Safety were created and spells of protection were put on them to save three young people from evil. Mary Beth Hamilton's *Amulet of Safety* is missing. Her granddaughter Eva Davis was careless and it is gone just when she needs it the most.

Mary Beth's Ghost appears to her granddaughter Eva and her friend Katherine to lead them to the missing amulet that has been hidden away. She tells them not to let anyone know it has been found so they can discover the real threat.

Learn how the talismans, and Grandmother's ghost play a part in the entwined lives of the Hamilton Family as they deal with death, truth, life and happiness, in this adventure set in the Regency Era, England.

OTHER CREDITS

- Janet was privileged to have a poem *Family Reunion*, included in an article by Mary Jo Fresch and David L. Harrison. *Playing with Poetry to Develop Phonemic Awareness* Printed in IRA Essentials, Motivating Readers, Inspiring Teachers. July 2013 issue.
- Sleuth's Ink Mystery Writers Anthology 2019 included a poem and two short stories by Janet Kay Gallagher

NOTE FROM THE AUTHOR

I hope you enjoyed reading You Must Believe Me as much as I enjoyed writing it. I'd appreciate it if you'd give it a review.

Thanks,
Janet Kay Gallagher